DROPPING IN WITH
andy mac
THE LIFE OF A PRO SKATEBOARDER

ANDY MACDONALD
WITH THERESA FOY DIGERONIMO

simon pulse
new york london toronto sydney singapore

First Simon Pulse edition May 2003

Text copyright © 2003 by Andy Macdonald

SIMON PULSE
An imprint of Simon & Schuster
Children's Publishing Division
1230 Avenue of the Americas
New York, NY 10020

Designed by Lauren Monchik
The text of this book was set in font DIN.

Printed in the United States of America
2 4 6 8 10 9 7 5 3

Library of Congress Control Number 2003100470

ISBN 0-689-85784-5

© 1992 Jeremy Traub

left: Body wrap lien to tail (the mummy) rockin' a
vintage Flyaway helmet and a Who Skates skateboard.

For my wife, Rebecca.
No matter what.

acknowledgments

thanks:

To my wife, Rebecca, for her unwavering love, commitment, and belief in me, and for her obsessive editing skills. To my family for years of undying love and support: Trudy Macdonald for introducing me to Gandhi and for instilling values in me that I still cherish today; Rod Macdonald for helping me realize my dream by teaching me relentless determination; Sharon Granger for her support; and Kyle Macdonald for being there to keep up with and for toughening me up. Also Joe Roman; Christian Boutwell; Chris "Rhino" Rooney; John "Bacon" Hobbs; Preston Maigetter; Dave Tuck; the Chang family; Koinonia Posse; Tony Hawk and the Hawk family; Powell and George and Julie Powell, Michael Furukawa; Andy Mac Skateboards; Airwalk and Bruce Pettet, and Shannon Hoffman; Andy Mac Shoes and Andy Mac Clothing; Swatch and Nadia Waelti; SoBe Beverages; LEGO-Bionicle; Harbinger; Pro-Tec; Flybar; John Flanagan; Chelsea Wilber; Barry Farber; Theresa DiGeronimo; Simon & Schuster and Julia Richardson; Chris Conway; Chris Miller; any skatepark that let me skate for free—past, present, future; everyone who has ever helped to get a public skateboard park built in their community; the United Professional Skateboarders Association and all of its members for helping to build a positive future for skateboarding; Mohandas K. Gandhi; David Dellinger; nonviolent revolutionaries; Nishi (the best puppy in the world); Honda Civics; candy; and kids everywhere.

table of contents

introduction

by Tony Hawk

Andy Macdonald is an example of perseverance. From early on, he knew he wanted to be a professional skateboarder—at a time when most of his peers considered it nothing more than a hobby. Some only dream of such a goal; Andy made it happen against great odds. He moved to California to follow his quest when making it big in skateboarding meant getting coverage in a few struggling magazines and meager paychecks. Obviously, money was not the motivating factor.

His early days in California were not rosy. He did odd jobs (like dressing up as Shamu at Sea World) while skating during every spare moment. Other skaters saw this devotion as uncool, like he was trying too hard in a sport that holds its uncaring rebels as heroes (as long as they skate well). His skating improved dramatically during his time on the West Coast, so much so that it was getting difficult for the most hard-core skaters to pass him off as a robotic jock (someone who can do many tricks but at minimum height). He became more powerful, invented highly technical tricks, and started going higher on his aerials. He caught a lot of flack for his so-called training schedule, but his skills were undeniable.

In 1996, Andy qualified for the second-ever X Games in Newport, Rhode Island, because of his consistent contest performances throughout the year. He was relatively unknown to people outside the skate industry coming to Newport, but everything changed that weekend: He won. The biggest televised skateboard event at that time, and he was considered the best. He also placed well in the street event, making him one of the few athletes who could conquer more than one style. He still had his naysayers, but the television audience that admired his skills without prejudice muffled their voices. Since 1997 his

left: Tony and I were skating doubles long before it became an event at the X Games. Indy airs to fakie for an old Airwalk ad.

name has been in the top ten placings in every contest.

I met Andy just before he moved to San Diego, and we have been skating together ever since. We have lived through too many ridiculous travel experiences (a.k.a. "hell trips"), like the time we weren't picked up at an airport in Zürich and were expected to get ourselves to a remote mountain three hours away, just to skate in subzero temperatures in a smoke-filled hall as a sideshow to a snowboard event. We have flown to Tokyo for a total stay of twenty hours, during which time we did two demos in freezing temperatures (so cold that I wore snow gloves while skating), bought new gadgets, and headed to the airport; we spent more time in the air than we did on the ground. Andy always approaches these situations with a good sense of humor and manages to rise to the occasion when expected to perform under such dire conditions. It is exactly the kind of attitude you need to live through our types of schedules, where we have intimate expertise on which airports have the best food and where jet lag is not an option once you arrive.

I have always admired Andy's devotion to skateboarding. He skates every chance he gets and always acts like a professional at any public exhibition or event. If you want someone to perform well on a crappy ramp, call Andy. If you want someone you can trust skating on the ramp with you at the same time (a.k.a. "doubles"), Andy is the man. If you need a headliner for a six-week, twenty-two-city arena tour (a.k.a. "Boom Boom Huck Jam"), you can rely on Andy to be at every show, arrive on time, work hard, and skate his best. Quite simply, the guy loves to skate, and he'll do whatever it takes to keep his dream of being a pro skater alive. He's also one of the best there is because he'll never give up.

left: Lester Kasai invented and named the benihana. Christian Hosoi perfected it and taught it to me when I was just a grom. It's still one of my favorite tricks.

part one:

back
in the
day

1.

from the start

For me, full speed was the only way to go.

It was one of the best days of my life. I had just won the vert competition at the 2000 NBC Gravity Games in Providence, Rhode Island, and everybody I loved was there to see it happen. My dad and stepmom, my mom, my aunts, uncles, and cousins, as well as my fiancée and her family were all there cheering for me. (I had sixteen guest passes that day, although I was supposed to have only two.) This was a really special day—not only because I won the competition, but also because my fiancée, Rebecca, and I had decided to have our engagement party that weekend. We wanted to introduce our families to each other. Even though there were thousands of people in the crowd that day, when I looked around, I easily spotted my large, extended family jumping up and down and waving their arms. I felt incredibly lucky to have so much support with me.

In the Beginning

On the day I was born, nobody would have guessed that twenty-seven years later we'd all be together. When my mother was eight months' pregnant, my parents split up. My father stayed behind in Nebraska, where they were living, and my mom moved with my brother, Kyle (who is three years older than me), to my aunt's home in Framingham, Massachusetts. Then, one month later, I was born in Natick, Massachusetts, at 11:00 A.M. on July 31, 1973. Soon after my birth my mom moved in with some friends in Peabody, Massachusetts, until she could find a place for us all to live.

This was a rocky start. My mom has told me that fortunately, I was a pretty laid-back baby and didn't mind the moves. In fact, I didn't even seem to notice that the three of us were living and sleeping together in one room.

Now here we all were at the Gravity Games. Some people might have found it awkward to have their divorced parents together at a skateboard contest and an engagement party. It didn't seem odd at all to me.

A Place Called Home

When I was one month old, my mom, my brother, and I moved to a rented duplex at 37 Teele Avenue in Somerville near Boston, and that's where my earliest memories kick in. It's funny that I can't remember my own phone number sometimes, but I've always remembered the address of that old yellow house with aluminum siding. It was just down the street from the Tufts University campus, and the neighborhood was full of college students (who never had candy to give out on Halloween, but who otherwise were pretty cool). I lived in that house until I was seven. What I didn't know at the time was that Somerville was a run-down town often called "Slumerville." All the houses sat really close to one another in this all-concrete area, and there were always shoes hanging from the power lines. But I didn't notice or care that we lived in one of the poorer Boston areas; Teele Avenue was a great place to live.

powdered milk

Money was pretty tight in those days, and although we laugh about it now, back then we couldn't afford real milk all the time. Instead, we always had a big box of powdered milk in the cupboard that had to be mixed up every day. If you were the one who finished the cold batch, you had to be the one to mix up more and put the container back in the fridge. If my brother or I forgot, we would get super bummed at each other because, although powdered milk is always terrible, warm powdered milk is even worse!

Constant Motion

My mother now had two little boys to care for by herself, so although she was a registered nurse, she stayed at home with us and opened a family day-care center. She took care of me and three other infants as well as my brother and one other toddler. Because I was so young, most of what I know about her day-care business comes from photos and stories from my mom. I'm sure that taking care of six little kids all day couldn't have been easy on her, especially since I was a pretty hyperactive kid—even as an infant.

Apparently, I was in constant motion. My mom swears I used to pull myself up to a standing position in my crib, grab hold of the upper bar, and do chin-ups. When I got a little older, I was always bouncing on Mom's bed (it had the best springs) and diving onto the couch in the living room. For me, full speed was the only way to go. Funny, though: I was so busy building muscle strength and coordination that I didn't put much effort into building verbal skills. I had nothing to say until I was about two years old. I was a spaz, but at least I was quiet.

Mom says that enrolling me in my first gymnastics class at age three was one of the best things she's ever done. But before I ever got to the gym, I was doing flips on my own. When I was nine months old, we had a jolly jumper in our kitchen—a seat

left: "He's not heavy, he's my brother!" Older brother Kyle holding fat little me.

that hung in a doorway on long springlike ropes that let babies bounce up and down. It was one of my favorite places to be. One day Mom put me in the jumper and left to take a shower. By the time she came out, I had bounced myself so high that I'd done a half-flip McTwist and was hanging upside down. I wasn't scared or crying; I was just chilling, checking out my new perspective on the world while my face turned purple.

My Poor Mom

My mom stayed home with us until I turned one, and then she got a job at a nearby hospital working nights. She hired a local college student named Tim to baby-sit Kyle and me while she was at work. Mom was always there for us in the day, which was probably a good thing, because as I grew I found more and more ways to get into trouble.

My poor mom counts three near poisonings before I was five years old. When I was about eighteen months old, we were visiting my aunt's house, and I discovered malathion (a deadly pesticide) in her garage. My mom says she came in and found me standing next to the broken malathion bottle with the smell of the pesticide on my breath. She called the poison control center, and the person who answered the phone said to give me ipecac syrup to make me vomit it up. That, thankfully, saved the day.

The next close call was when I was three years old. We were up in New Hampshire at a cookout, and the host used kerosene to start the barbecue. It wasn't long before my mother found me holding the can of kerosene with the smell of it on my breath. This time the poison control center rep (my mom had memorized the phone number by now) said that I should drink milk and be watched carefully for any seizures or signs of serious illness. Again I pulled through.

The near poisoning that I was old enough to remember was when I was three and got my hands on a brand-new bottle of children's chewable vitamins with fluoride shaped like the Flintstone characters. (This was before child safety caps were

right: I used to skate these three stairs behind Ceritani's supermarket in Melrose all day long. This was the first handrail I ever slid.

invented.) My friend Matt and I hid behind the couch and ate the whole bottle before my mom found us. Fortunately, my mom never panicked over my adventures. This time she calmly broke out the ipecac syrup, and in no time Matt and I were puking little bits of Fred and Barney all over the bathroom and Mom still made it to work on time.

I remember one night I really hurt myself, and my mom wasn't so calm. It was a cold winter night, and my brother and I were riding home in the back of Mom's Ford Pinto. It was late, but she had promised that when we got home, we could stay up for a cup of hot Ovaltine. I was the first one in the house, and after a quick change into my PJs I ran into the kitchen to help prepare the treat. I opened the bottom cabinet door and used it as a step to jump up on the countertop to get my favorite Peter Rabbit mug from the top shelf. With mug in hand, I pushed off to jump down backward and caught the inside of my groin on the corner of the cabinet door that I had left open. I landed on my butt on the floor and assessed the situation. I was looking at a four-inch-long gash. It was a pretty deep cut, but it didn't hurt much. I casually called for my mother.

This time my mother did panic. Being a nurse, she knew that the cut was very close to the femoral artery. If I had cut into that, I could have bled to death in about thirty seconds. She shouted directions to my brother—something about some towels—as she picked me up and headed out the door.

My mother is usually an overly cautious driver. There are, however, two situations in which she transforms into a NASCAR racer: when she's late for church and when she's rushing to the hospital. It's really amazing that Mom didn't plow anyone down as she blew through red lights and took tight corners at top speed. I remember that she was concentrating so hard on her driving that she wasn't talking. My brother kept asking why he had to sit in the backseat pressing on my wound with all his weight. But there was no answer. It wasn't until later that my mother explained how close to death I had come.

It seems that most of my early childhood memories landed me in the hospital. As I grew older and was able to take my extra energy outside on my own, the fun (and the trouble) multiplied.

2.

smash yourself

From the earliest age, I've had a fascination with anything that can result in bodily harm.

A psychologist doing a report on X Games athletes once diagnosed me as a natural-born risk taker. He said that the only way I can feel like I'm really living is to come close to dying. I don't completely agree. I feel like I'm really living when I'm sitting in front of a big, fat Ben & Jerry's ice-cream sundae, and that's hardly death defying. But I do admit that from the earliest age, I've had a fascination with anything that can result in bodily harm, and I did seem to find a way to defy death more often than my mother would have liked.

The Screech of Tires

Most often the trouble began when I was trying to keep up with my older brother. When I was four years old, I had a Big Wheel bike that, in my mind, was pretty much the same as the Harley that my hero, Evel Knievel, rode when he went for one of his

daredevil jumps. My brother and I had the Evel Knievel doll that came with the crank-up motorcycle launch. We'd build a jump at the top of a set of ten stairs with no landing ramp, crank the motorcycle up as fast as it could go, and let him rip. We'd yell, "He can do it! He's Evel!" Like Evel, I used to jump my Big Wheel off the curb into the street so often that, eventually, the whole thing just broke in half.

One day while out riding, my friend Matt was chasing me at top speed down the sidewalk. I opted for some evasive maneuvers by busting my patented curb launch. Just as I hit the street and pulled the skid brake, setting me into a sweet 180, I heard the sound of rubber tires skidding. *Wow!* I thought. *My Big Wheel doesn't usually make such a cool sound.* As I came around on my 180, I saw the grill of a Cadillac coming straight for my face. With a high-pitched screech, it stopped a few inches from my nose. The driver jumped out of his car in a panic. I'm sure he thought he'd killed me. When he saw that I was okay, he probably wanted to kill me for almost getting killed. He was furious. My mom wasn't home, so Matt's poor father had to deal with the crazed Caddy driver when he stormed up to the door with me under one arm and Matt under the other.

The Kyle-and-Andy Daredevil Duo

By the age of five I knew the feeling I got from an adrenaline rush, and I wanted to keep it coming. One summer my brother got a Huffy Street Machine bike for his birthday. It wasn't long before he was bombing down "Taa Hill" over on the Tufts University campus. ("Taa Hill" is simply what we kids with our Boston accents called the tar walkway that led down the hill from campus to the dorms.) On this same hill there was a sidewalk where some of the cement squares had been pushed up by the roots of an old oak tree. It made a natural launch ramp for "wicked awesome" jumps.

In no time big brother Kyle was asking for volunteers to lay down in front of the "Kyle kicker." Jimmy got conned into doing it. Jimmy was a really skinny kid from across the street who looked like he had never seen a Hostess Twinkie. Because he

left: My brother and I on top of Hadley's ramp.

was so skinny, everybody thought Kyle could easily jump over him. But just before Kyle and his Street Machine reached the jump, Jimmy got scared and rolled out of harm's way. Boy, was Kyle angry. While he was busy calling Jimmy a wimp, I saw my opportunity. I lay down next to the twisted sidewalk and waited. "See? Even little Andy's not scared!" Kyle yelled, jumping back on his bike. "I'll jump him instead." Jimmy picked up a rock and began to write on the nearby cement. He wrote down a disclaimer that relieved him of having to pay any hospital bills for my brother or me in the event of a disaster. I wonder if skinny Jimmy became a lawyer.

Of course the Kyle-and-Andy daredevil duo pulled off the stunt with flying colors and were the talk of the block for weeks. Mom wasn't nearly as impressed when she found out about it. She took away the Street Machine for a week or two, but it wasn't long before we were back in business.

like no other feeling in the world

When I reminded my mom of the Street Machine story, she looked puzzled and asked, "Don't you have any *good* memories of your childhood?" I have many positive traits that I attribute to my mother, but having the courage to lie down in front of an oncoming bike is not one of them. I had to explain to her that these *are* my good childhood memories. It's hard to describe to someone like my mother the feeling I get from coming close to harm and getting away with it. When I'm skating in a contest, I'll risk slamming or getting hurt because if I pull off the trick, it's like no other feeling in the world. Often I find myself screaming as I roll away from the landing. I don't know whether it's because I'm scared to death or because I'm so happy to be standing. Maybe it's a little of both. Whatever it is, it's a rush every time, and I love it. These are the moments of my good memories.

It's Not My Fault

Though many people blame their parents for the way they turned out, I'm going to blame my brother. Whatever childhood lunacy didn't come to me naturally, I learned from watching him and his friends.

above: Classic New England style: smashed board, sketchy launch ramp, snow on the ground, jumping over my friends.

Kyle's friend John had a bike with one of those long "banana" seats that could fit two riders. Every once in a while the two of them would send out a call: "Feed bags!" It had become a Teele Avenue tradition. Every kid in the neighborhood would scatter looking for some change. I'd hit my piggy bank and find maybe seventy-five cents that I'd saved from my allowance. Then we'd all come running back with a list of candy we wanted my brother and John to get from the store. My favorites were red licorice shoelaces and a hard candy called Fizz that had a fizzy center. Up and down the street you could hear kids yelling, "I want a Fun Dip and five purple fish!" "I want two Hostess cupcakes!" "I want three freezey pops!" and on and on until all the lists and money had been collected. Then Kyle and John would ride off on John's bike to the store as fast as they could. I don't know why they had to go so fast, but that was part of "feed bags day."

The rest of us would sit on the curb and wait for their return. It was like waiting for the opening of some great show because it was on the return trip where the dangers lay. On the way to the store *up* the hill my brother could hold on to John's waist and get there safely, but on the ride home John would come cranking *down* the hill at top speed and then have to turn onto Teele Ave., taking the corner way too tightly and cutting across two lanes of oncoming traffic. My brother would be behind John, legs out for balance, holding on to the bags of soda and junk food with both arms and no way to steady himself on the bike. We'd take bets on whether they could make the turn without crashing. I'd always bet that my brother wouldn't drop the bags, because he had a great dismount that could save him every time. At just the right moment he would scoot off the back of the bike and land in a run. It was great to watch. Thanks to my brother, I had a rich appreciation for danger at a young age.

Playing in the Streets

When I was about six years old, I was playing football on the street with my brother and his friends, who were nine or ten. This "toughens you up" quick. That's what my brother would say when he was beating on me: "I'm toughening you up. You should thank me!"

right: Frontside air at Hadley's.

The real fun came when someone would call for a game of Relievio (better known in most neighborhoods as "chase"). We usually played after dinner in the summer for a few hours before twilight. Every kid in the neighborhood was expected to play. I, being one of the youngest and smallest, saw it as an opportunity to prove that I could hang with the big kids. We'd split up into two teams, set boundaries, and designate someone's front porch as the jail. One team hid and the other gave chase. In order to be caught, a person from the opposing team had to grab you, hold on, and count out, "One, two, three, Relievio," and then you were taken to jail. To be freed, one of your teammates had to touch the front stairs of the porch/jail and say, "Relievio!" Everyone in jail would then be free. Some games of Relievio would last a week; each team would write down who was captive and who was free at the end of an evening's session.

A jailbreak wasn't as easy as it sounds, though. Once there were prisoners, there would be a guard. Oftentimes freeing your team-mates meant sacrificing your own freedom—or your own body. Every once in a while I'd be lucky enough to get a chance to free one of the big kids, and it was worth every bump and bruise. The best Relievio player ever was crazy Allen. He was about four years older than me. He had a tangled mop of scraggly black hair, and he was lanky and athletic. The greatest thing about him was that he didn't much care what happened to his body. Everyone seemed to have a special reverence toward Allen as the king of Relievio. To be picked to be on his team was an honor. Allen was the hero who was almost always the last to be caught and the first to free his team.

Once when I was on Allen's team, our whole team had been caught, except, of course, for Allen. Someone on the porch saw Allen come sprinting out from between two houses about halfway down the block. Only a few strides behind him were three members of the opposing team. We all gathered at the top of the stairs, cheering him on and hoping to be freed. Our jail guard left his post to cut off Allen's angle at the stairs. Without breaking stride, Allen jumped onto the hood of a parked car and continued running toward us. Up onto the roof, down the back, and onto the next car he went. By then he had bypassed the jail guard and was back on the street. He ran across the sidewalk and right up the stairs yelling, "Relievio!" and sending his team scattering off in all directions. Being the littlest one, I was quickly caught with a clothesline-style stiff arm from one of Allen's pursuers.

As I lay there trying to get the air back in my lungs, I realized the predicament Allen was in. The porch's rail was a good six feet above the ground. He had backed himself in and was now facing three of his would-be captors. But Allen wasn't going out like that. He took a quick look over his shoulder, and without any hesitation, dove headfirst into the thicket of thornbushes behind him. He hit the ground with a thud but scrambled to his feet and was over the neighbor's fence and gone before the other guys knew what had happened. I couldn't believe what I'd just seen!

When Allen circled back, everyone gathered around him to check out his shredded clothing and bloody arms and chest. We congratulated him on the best jailbreak in Teele Avenue history. Crazy Allen was the best! He was always unfazed by the punishment his body took. I wanted to be just like him someday.

3.

new kid in town

This was my first opportunity to try out Gandhi's philosophy of nonviolence.

We moved away from Teele Avenue when I was seven years old, in the middle of second grade. My mom had bought her own duplex in Melrose, a town just twenty minutes north of Somerville. Melrose was a much nicer place than Somerville, with its trees and parks, but I didn't care. I didn't want to leave my friends or the neighborhood that I'd grown up in. But usually kids don't have the last say.

Along with the move came the typical problems that come with being the new kid in town. I was now going to a large public school (rather than the private Catholic school I was used to in Somerville), and everything seemed so different.

The Bully

Friends didn't come right away. Before I met any of my new second-grade buddies, the class bully decided he wanted to fight me. I was walking home from school one day when I noticed that I was being followed by a group of kids. Apparently, word had gotten around to everyone but me that the new kid was going to get beat up, so everyone was waiting for the fight to start. The bully, who was leading the crowd, came up to me and started pushing me around, trying to get me to fight him. He dumped my books out of my hands, and I picked them up and kept walking. He pushed me into the bushes and I got up and kept walking. He did this again and again, and I just kept ignoring him. We were approaching the end of the block where I would make a turn to go to my house. Since he had to walk straight to get to his house, I was hoping he'd just keep going—but what this really meant was that he had to make his move before I turned.

He jumped on my back and tackled me to the ground. He threw a couple punches to my ribs but didn't do much damage. To defend myself, I used some moves I'd learned from years of wrestling my older brother and got him pinned down so he was flat on his back with my knees on his arms. He couldn't move, and I could have started pounding on him. I was so mad, I really did want to hit him. But I didn't.

This was my first opportunity to try out Gandhi's philosophy of nonviolence. My mom had taught me about nonviolence being a weapon of the strong, and here was my chance to prove it. I made a fist, held it right to his face, and hollered, "You're not one of my favorite people right now, but I'm not fighting you, so you can leave me alone." I got up, kicked his book bag, and walked away. After that he didn't bother me anymore. I learned that day that although there are definitely things worth fighting for, it's not necessary to use violence in order to win.

Best Friends

Soon after the "fight" with the school bully I met a kid who is still a good friend of mine. Jody Roman was in my class and on my soccer team and was also new in town. One of the first things we noticed about each other was that we both had the exact same red-and-silver Huffy Pro-Thunder BMX bikes and we were psyched on them. We would ride to soccer practice every day and try to do jumps like I saw my older brother and his friends do back in Somerville. Right away we were best friends.

Our friendship was strong enough that it continued even when Jody moved on to third grade and I was held back in second. My verbal skills were still a bit behind everyone else's, and I was a slow reader. After moving away from my friends on Teele Avenue, I didn't feel much like trying to improve academically, so things had gotten worse. My teacher and my mother thought it would be a good idea to try second grade again; I wasn't so sure.

In my second year of second grade I had to make classroom friends all over again. I was drawn to a boy named Brian Ackerman, who was also very quiet. It turns out Brian was a good choice as a second-grade friend. His family was wealthier than all the others, so he always had the best toys and the best sugary snacks in town. Nobody ever wanted to come to my house for snacks because my mother was into healthy foods. For Easter my brother and I would get carob bunnies rather than chocolate. All we ever had was what we called "sticks and twigs"—really just things like granola and dried fruit—no match for the drawer full of Hostess cakes and Twix bars at Brian's house. Brian, Jody, and I all lived within three blocks of one another, and by the middle of the year we were a tight group of friends.

work ethic

My mom sure knew how to teach her boys to work for what they wanted. One winter when I was about nine years old, Mom said she was willing to *take* us to the mountains to go downhill skiing but not to *pay* for any of it. Kyle had a paper route at the time, so it was a cinch for him to pay for his ski gear, gather his friends together, and hire Mom's taxi service to drive them up to Vermont for the day. I, on the other hand, was too young for a paper route, or any other job for that matter, so I got left behind. This experience sparked my quest for financial independence and, more immediately, downhill skiing.

I was so determined in my quest that I hardly noticed the sweatshop wages I earned from my mother. Chores and challenges—sweeping the stairs, vacuuming the rugs, raking the yard, shoveling the driveway, washing the windows, and cleaning out the basement—were all met head on. I had a goal, and I was going to see it through!

Finally, the day arrived. I had worked for two months straight, saving every penny. I proudly dished out $25 for a pair of used skis, pitched in my share for gas, and hopped in the "Mom Cab" with my brother and his friends. Once we were at the mountain, the fact that I had no idea how to ski didn't matter. My brother put me on the chairlift headed for the summit, and I couldn't have been happier. I had worked so hard to get there. I was going downhill skiing!

War and Peace

From second grade, when I moved to Melrose, until sixth grade, when I found skateboarding, my days were spent outside with the neighborhood kids. A game we played often was called "Guns." Probably because my mother wouldn't let us have toy guns, not even squirt guns, it was one of my favorite things to do. Brian had all the biggest and best toy guns around—like A-Team rifles and Miami Vice magnums—and he was happy to share with us. Across from Brian's house was a wooded area with rocks and boulders that we would climb on and hide behind while shooting one another. I would get way too into it, tying grass to my head and body for camouflage. We'd chase each other around all after-noon, yelling, "Boom! You're gone!" "No way! I shot you first. You've gotta fall down and count to thirty!" "No I don't! I'm not dead!" No one ever won, but that wasn't the point anyway.

At the same time I was toting those guns and aiming to kill, I was doing book reports on Gandhi's method of peaceful resist-ance and still following his guiding philosophy of nonviolence. I was really a pacifist at heart, but playing Guns was just so much fun. Besides, nobody was getting hurt.

Summers with Dad

By the time I was in second grade, I was spending my summers in Michigan with my dad. From the day school let out in June until the beginning of September, my brother and I lived with Dad and his new wife, Sharon, in Ann Arbor. (Actually, I call her "Sharon #1" because his current wife is named Sharon too.) My brother and I stayed pretty much to ourselves while Dad was at work. We'd keep each other company playing long and very

competitive games of one-on-one Wiffle ball and Frisbee golf in the back of my dad's apartment complex.

For one week every summer we went to a sports day camp on the campus of the University of Michigan. Kyle picked baseball camp, and I chose gymnastics. I spent the whole week in gymnastics camp working on a routine on the high bar that I'd perform on the last day in front of all the parents. The day of the performance, with my dad and all the other parents looking on, my routine started perfectly. I even remembered to point my toes. The finish to my program would be a "flyaway" dismount. I had done it a million times. I got into a handstand above the bar. All I had to do was swing around under the bar, and on my way up again I would let go of the bar, letting my momentum carry me into a back flip and land . . . perfectly! But this time I held on too long on my way up and didn't "fly away" soon enough. As I came around I caught both of my shins on the bar and landed flat on my stomach, eight feet below on the mat. It hurt my ego more than my body. I literally fell on my face in front of everyone.

This was the first time I felt like I'd really failed. I had always been one of the best in every sport I'd tried up to that point, and this was my first lesson in sporting failure. I'd let my pop down, and it felt terrible. Of course, Dad didn't see it that way. But it was hard to find out I could make mistakes. Years later I'd be reminded of this lesson at the 1997 X Games vert contest when I didn't even make the cut.

Charlie Don't Surf

For the rest of the summer in Michigan my brother and I just played our backyard games and waited for Dad's vacation from work. Vacation meant packing ourselves like sardines into Dad's 1979 Honda Civic and driving to Flagler Beach, Florida, to visit my father's parents for two weeks. We had to drive two ten-hour days each way, but it was worth it. I really liked hanging out with my grandma and grandpa, and there was never a boring moment at the beach.

My grandparents' house was an easy walk to the Atlantic

left: Our first halfpipe was eight feet wide and had PVC pipe cut in half and nailed on for coping. It's where I did my first invert.

Ocean, where my brother and I spent most of our time during the visits. We would often take a four-person, blow-up raft out into the waves and see if we could stay in it. My brother and I would sit up in the bow, and my dad would swim us out to where the biggest waves were breaking. He'd get the boat into the impact zone and then shove us into the crest just as the wave got to vert. We'd go flying! If his timing was off, the whole raft would flip over and we'd be swimming with the fishes. I was so little that sometimes I would just be holding my breath going through the washing machine until Dad would grab me and stand me up. I'd be coughing and trying to catch my breath, half scared but still laughing my head off.

The real fun began when Grandpa bought my brother and me Styrofoam belly boards. They were really cheap ones that didn't have fins or leashes. They were meant for just resting belly-down and coasting in on the waves, but my brother and I immediately turned them into surfboards. Although learning how to surf was fun at first, a couple of incidents made me start to change my mind about the joys of the ocean.

My brother and I were out past the breakers one time when I took a spill. Because my board didn't have a leash, I had to swim over to get it back. As I got closer to the board the water around me suddenly got really choppy and swirly. I was treading water, and before I could move, I was in the middle of a school of bluefish. They're big, about ten to twelve inches long, and they have really sharp teeth. They were knocking into my legs, and all I could think about was a stupid movie we had just seen, *Piranha II: The Spawning*, about killer flying fish that attack your neck. Just as I reached my board a big fish jumped out of the water and over my left shoulder. He smacked his tail on my forehead before diving back in. I jumped on my board, screaming, and paddled back to shore as fast as I could. It was a couple days before I got the guts up to head into deep water again. It wasn't until the next incident a few summers later that I finally decided surfing wasn't for me.

The water was pretty rough that day, but I knew I could handle

right: Ripping the Flagler Beach, Florida, shore break in 1978.

it. I paddled out and almost immediately got caught by the lip of a wave that knocked me off my board. Underwater and completely disoriented, I started swimming hard to get to the surface . . . when my head hit the sandy bottom! Wrong way! I was almost out of breath as I turned around and swam up and up as hard as I could. Every minute seemed like an hour, and I thought I would never reach the surface. By the time I came up, the current had carried me a couple hundred yards down the beach and I had inhaled a bunch of water. My dad, realizing what was happening, ran, following me down the beach, until I finally got to shore. He sat with me while I puked up seawater and swore I'd never surf again.

When I moved out to San Diego, that was a hard promise to keep. Everybody out there surfed and pushed me to join them. I went a few times, but it wasn't really surfing—it was more like swimming around with a surfboard attached to my ankle. I can catch a wave now and then, but in general, I stick to the boards that have wheels under them.

Winter Fun

Wintertime back with Mom was also full of adventures, especially when Brian, Jody, and I were together. The three of us would go up to Brian's family's cottage in New Hampshire and ride around in the snow on three-wheeled Honda ATCs. They're banned now because they're so easy to tip, but back then you didn't need a license or anything to use them. We'd gun it around on the frozen lake, cranking the wheel and doing donuts, kicking snow up at one another.

One time I went for a hard turn with way too much speed. As I went to put my foot down to stop from tipping over, my pant leg got caught in the back wheel, pulling me off and under the bike. Luckily, I sank into the snow as the ATC ran over my legs. As soon as the bike passed, I jumped up and looked myself over, hoping I was all still there. My body was fine, but my pants were torn from the ankle to the crotch. Jody and Brian came riding up to me. I expected them to say, *Are you okay? We thought you were finished!* But instead, they just burst out laughing—they could see my underwear, and there was nothing funnier than that.

Head Spins

In 1984, when I was in fifth grade, my friends and I got super into break dancing. We would bring a big sheet of cardboard or linoleum with our boom box down to the basketball courts almost every day of the week to practice. My friend Brendan and I used to do doubles, and we'd work on a routine for hours. We started one dance by running right at each other and doing front handsprings. We'd do back spins, head spins, and windmills. Whenever I could fit it in, I'd run up a wall and do a back flip. The gymnastic lessons I had been taking since I was three were really coming in handy!

On Saturday nights we'd go over to Roller World for break-dancing "battles." That was the day when they'd turn one of their smaller rinks into a space just for break-dancers. Different groups from different towns would take turns outdoing one another. I really liked it because break dancing was both physical and competitive.

When I was a kid, it didn't matter if it was sunny or snowing, I was always running around, and I was usually outside. I didn't watch much TV or play board games, and at that time there were no home computers and really no video games worth my time. I had too much energy just to sit around so these activities couldn't hold my attention for long. It wasn't until I discovered skateboarding that I knew I had found something that I could focus on and never get bored with. From that point on everything else in my life came second to skating.

part two:
skatepark
kid

4.
my first skateboard
Possessed to skate

When I watch other pro skateboarders at a session, I'm always amazed. It takes incredible strength and determination for guys to take slam after slam and still get up and try their tricks again. We have all practiced our skills for years—usually since we were young kids. I guess that's why I never understood why when I was in school, athletes like football players and basketball players put down skaters. We were all interested in the same thing: challenging our bodies and pushing our limits, trying to be the best.

A Jock from the Start

From the time of my first gymnastics class at age three, I have always been involved in sports and have always done pretty well in them. When I was in grade school, I wrestled at the YMCA with kids who were usually older and bigger than me. In soccer

I was the center halfback; in basketball I was the point guard; and on the swim team I swam the 100-meter breaststroke, the 100-meter backstroke, and the 200-meter individual medley relay (back, butterfly, breast, and freestyle in the same race). Although I played a lot of neighborhood football, my mom wouldn't let me play on the football team because she thought it was too dangerous.

Of all the sport events in grade school, I especially remember my soccer games. Each member of our team from working-class Melrose was given a T-shirt as our entire official uniform. We'd play teams from more affluent towns that had the whole deal—Umbro shorts, matching socks, shin guards, and soccer jerseys with the players' names and numbers on them. I can't say we didn't care. We wanted Umbro shorts and shiny soccer jerseys too. It was intimidating seeing the other team roll up in its own bus wearing full uniforms—and with cheerleaders to boot. There is a lot to be said for looking like you know what you're doing; they had that part covered. But in the end, I think our situation helped us. We played that much harder because we were the underdogs from the start. Life is funny like that. When people make negative assumptions about you, you can either take it in and believe they're right, or else you can fight to prove them wrong.

Although I didn't compete on a team, I continued my gymnastics lessons on and off over the years. Now I wish I had taken it more seriously. On the vert ramp skateboarding is gymnastics on wheels. This is especially true when you're in the air. You need good air sense to know which way is up and to wind up on your feet after a flip. Rob Boyce (a.k.a. "Sluggo") is a pro skater who's still an avid gymnast. He's never scared to get upside down on the vert ramp. He knows exactly where he is at all times, so he never panics.

I no longer practice gymnastics at the gym, but I do use the trampoline in my backyard. Although this helps me build air sense, there are still times when I get upside down on a ramp and freak out.

I discovered skateboarding in sixth grade, and everything changed. I started giving up other sports so I'd have more time to skate. First I quit wrestling and the swim team. Then I quit

© Brittain

soccer and basketball. Jody convinced me to swim again for the school team in my junior year of high school (and I got a varsity letter for it), but by then I was over team sports. My whole life focus shifted to skateboarding.

First Skateboard Sighting

I was three years old the first time I ever saw a skateboard. My brother and I both celebrate our birthdays in July, so Mom used to have one big birthday party for both of us. Kyle was turning six that year, and his big present was his first-ever skateboard. It was a blue plastic GT banana board, about four inches wide, with a kick tail and the newest-in-technology urethane wheels. Kyle was so excited about the new board that he ran straight to the driveway to try it out, and I ran after him to watch. He threw his shirtless belly down on the board and pushed off, but before he even got halfway down the driveway, he hit a rock. The board stopped, and Kyle kept right on going, skidding on his stomach across our chunky gravel-and-asphalt driveway. When he stood up, he was one big nasty scrape from his chin to his belly button. Mom put the board away, and it didn't come out for a long time after that.

I must have been about five or six when that old skateboard found its way out of the toy box. We didn't really know what skateboarding was at that time, but we found ways to have fun anyway. This was when we were back in Somerville and we'd play on "Taa Hill." We'd stand on the board up at the top and try to stay on all the way to the bottom. That was pretty much as far as we got with skateboarding back then, but we'd spend the whole day doing it.

When this got too boring, my brother and I would use the board for "street water-skiing." We would tie a stick to a piece of rope and use it as a towline. Then we'd tie the end to the back of Kyle's Huffy. The street was water, and the sidewalks were the docks. I usually wanted to play the part of the water-skier, and my brother didn't seem to mind dragging me around, so it worked out well.

left: In 1997 I won the High Air contest in Las Vegas, Nevada, despite critics who said I never went high enough.

My Own Board

I was twelve years old and in sixth grade before I saw another skateboard. It happened one night in early December when I was at Gooch Park, right around the corner from my house. I was rocking some sweatpants folded up on my shins with knee-high socks and two hooded sweatshirts to stay warm. Brian and I were shooting some hoops when one of the neighborhood kids came rolling by on a brand-new board. It was huge compared to the only skateboard I'd ever seen. I asked to try it out and was immediately hooked.

This board was so much smoother than my brother's old GT. It was about ten inches wide, with big, stable trucks and fat, soft wheels that had sealed precision bearings. I thought it was the easiest thing in the world to ride because of its size. Within minutes, I was walking up and down it and spinning pirouettes. I even did my first 360 that night by rolling backward up to the post of the basketball hoop, grabbing on and pulling myself around it. I didn't want to give the board back—I was possessed to skate.

Brian and I both went home that night and began nagging our parents for skateboards for Christmas. Brian got his right away (and, luckily, shared with me). But my mom had a different idea about Christmas presents. After a couple weeks of nagging her, she took me to Caldor's department store. I looked through all the boards, checking out the different wheels and graphics. Finally, I chose a Variflex Twister board because I liked the shape and the graphics. The boards back then didn't have an upkick nose; they had only an inch of rounded nose above the front truck and then the board came straight back down the rails with a squared-off, kicked-up tail. But this board was different; it had a fish shape. As the rails came down it got thinner just before the tail and then got wider again. The graphics were purple-and-white checks in a swirl, like a funnel twister. It cost about $80. My mom bought it, brought it home, and locked it in the attic until Christmas.

Those were a long couple of weeks before I finally got the board. When I did get it on Christmas morning, I couldn't even use it because we were at Aunt Margie's house and there was a foot of snow on the ground. But for the rest of the winter I skated some in my garage, and whenever weather allowed, I shoveled the snow off the driveway, hoping it would be dry by the next day. (I looked like the Pillsbury Doughboy skating in all my layers of sweatpants and flannel shirts.) But I didn't really get riding seriously until the weather began to break in late February.

Skate Lessons

The following March my brother got a hand-me-down board from one of his high school friends. It was an old Madrid that was beat up, but it was a pro model board, not a starter one like my Variflex. It was through these older kids that I learned about real skateboarding. One of the kids had a four-foot-wide quarter pipe in his driveway, and my brother would come home and tell me stories about it. These guys also gave me my first look at a skate magazine—it was *Thrasher*, and Tony Hawk was on the cover doing an airwalk. I couldn't believe it. Not only was he flying in the air, but both feet were off his board. I had never seen anything like this. There was so much more about skateboarding that I had to learn.

I started my "lessons" at the C-Bowl in Cambridge. This was the first out-of-town spot I heard about through my brother's friends. The C-Bowl was a public swimming pool with a thirteen-foot deep end that was empty during the off-season. It was an hour's train ride away, but that didn't bother me. I had been taking the train into Boston by myself to visit my orthodontist since fourth grade—and this was far better than going to the dentist.

As a grom I took a lot of slams in that pool. My brother remembers standing in the shallow end and watching me head down toward the deep end. He'd lose sight of me as I dropped down, and then he'd see the board come flying up after I slammed. I still wasn't wearing any pads or a helmet, but I was determined to get this right no matter how much it hurt. Eventually, I learned a lot at the C-Bowl. It had a huge kink with three feet of vert above it, and this is where I did my first backside grind. It was just a little kick turn grind, but I was so stoked.

Tight-Knit Group

Right after I got my board at Christmas, it seemed like the whole sixth-grade class got boards too. It was the "in" thing to do. We would just cruise around town on our boards. Of course, we didn't really know what skateboarding was, but everyone who was anyone was doing it.

Jody and I had met a kid named Christian Boutwell in fifth grade, and he started skating with us. The three of us continued skating even when we started junior high in seventh grade and skateboarding wasn't cool anymore—but it wasn't easy. The principal took our boards away on the first day. He met us at the front steps and said with great authority, "You're not allowed to skate on school property. You can pick up your boards in my office at the end of the day. And don't ever bring them back here again." It didn't take us long to find a back entrance where we could sneak the boards in and hide them in our lockers before anybody saw us.

Because there weren't too many kids who skated, those of us who did quickly became a tight-knit group. If I was skating by City Hall in downtown Melrose and heard wheels coming down the street, I'd turn around. Even if I didn't know who it was, I'd skate over and introduce myself because I wanted to know all the skaters. I found it easy to talk to kids I'd never met before simply because they skated.

This was unusual in Melrose, which was divided in half by railroad tracks. The kids on my side of the tracks rarely talked to the rich kids on the other side. But one day at a street fair we met a bunch of kids who came skating down from Melrose Highlands. There was no tension or hesitation; Chris, Brian, Rich, Andy, and Scott immediately became our friends. We hooked up and became the "Melrose Skate Gang" (later we called ourselves "Local Chaos"). It was the love for skateboarding that bonded us. The more I travel, the more I see that this special camaraderie of skateboarders exists all over the world.

Skating Boston

It wasn't long before we were looking for bigger and better places to skate. Nearby Boston was a natural choice for street skating, with lots of concrete, walls, and stairs to conquer. Almost every weekend we'd follow the same loop around town:

right: In '98 I won the Transworld Reader's Poll Best All Around Skater award. This is the photo they used.

- We'd start at what we called "Metals." This was a large metal art sculpture at the busy intersection of New Chardon and Congress Streets. To us, it was a perfectly smooth twenty-foot-wide ramp on a thirty-five-degree angle. You could skate up it from the sidewalk, or you could come from across the intersection and time your run with the changing of the streetlight. This was our first-stop meeting place. There were always other skaters there that we'd hook up with.

- From Metals, we'd all go over to the train station at Boston City Hall. On the sides of the stairs that led to the station were brick walls on eighty-degree angles. Although it was a bumpy ride on brick, we'd do wallrides about four or five feet up. We'd also skate the stairs for a while before moving on down Beacon Street.

- On Beacon we'd skate right by the graves of John Hancock, Paul Revere, and Samuel Adams. This area was always filled with tourists who seemed annoyed when we skated through their tour group, but we were just passing through and never hurt anybody. Living on the West Coast now, which has no comparable landmarks, I now appreciate all the history I skated past in Boston.

- The Boston Public Gardens, a huge field with cement walkways crisscrossing through it, was our next stop. There'd be people all over the place, but that didn't bother us. We'd go "people skating," using them like slalom cones and skating around them. We never ran into anyone, but occasionally, we had to dive onto the grass to avoid it. We were in control.

- We'd leave the Public Garden, skate down Newbury Street (an upper-class shopping area), and go over to the Prudential Center. This skyscraper had a reflection pool out front that was emptied in cooler weather. It had banked walls that we skated until the security staff kicked us out.

- Next we'd move down Massachusetts Avenue to Roxbury. It wasn't the best neighborhood, but it had one of the best places to skate. At one of the entrances to Boston City Hospital were huge brick volcano-like structures. One was thirteen feet high and the other was six feet high. They had smooth transitions with a two-foot-wide deck at the top. Basically, they were two quarter pipes. All around the hospital there were brick banks and wedges and stairs that were great for skating. We spent hours there and joked about the fact that if anybody got hurt, the hospital was right there!

- Farther down the street was the "Black Hole." This was my first experience with drainage ditches. It was a black tar ditch filled with sewage, trash, and junk. It wasn't very deep, but it was long. After sweeping it out, you could start at the top and carve back and forth like a snake run. Other skaters would bring parking blocks and pieces of plywood and edge them up on the sides. So among the reeds and sewer rats we had our own little skatepark. We'd get out of there as soon as it started getting dark. It wasn't the best place to be at night if you weren't from there.

At the end of the day we'd jump on the train and head back home.

it wasn't always a crime

When I first started street skating in Boston, it was pretty hassle-free. The sport wasn't so popular, and there weren't too many kids using public land for their skating. We also weren't yet into sliding down handrails or jumping big stairs. It was more about flowing and carving and jumping off some ledges and riding some banks. We were lucky that we could skate without being called a "problem." Today, Metals is still at that intersection, but you won't see any skaters around it. The city ripped up the cement sidewalk there and put in cobblestones, making it unridable. But kids still managed to skate it, so the sculpture was moved across the street and an iron fence was put up around it. Boston City Hospital is still one of the best places to skate in Boston, but security has been beefed up and now kids are chased away as soon as they get there. But hassles like these don't discourage skaters. We're still all out there, always scouting for new places to skate.

Jocks vs. Skaters

In eighth grade I wasn't a jock anymore; I was becoming a skateboarder. I wore different clothes, grew my hair long, and hung around with other skateboarders in the school (all five of them). When we were skating in Boston, we'd stop at a thrift store to do clothes shopping. At the time we were into the punk-rock scene. We were listening to bands like Gang Green, Slapshot, and Minor Threat. We'd buy the cheesiest, old-man plaid pants for two bucks and cut them into shorts. These matched with ripped, old T-shirts, a flannel shirt over it buttoned only on the top button, and Converse Chuck Taylor All Stars. To finish the look, I got a flop haircut like Tony Hawk's and Kevin Staab's: hair parted on the side, my bangs down to the bottom of my chin, and the back and sides of my head shaved.

I was finding out who I really was and, at the same time, finding out who my friends were. Now that I wasn't shooting hoops or playing neighborhood football anymore, my old friends tried to put me down. Guys who just a year before were my bros now tried to humiliate me whenever they got a chance. They would drive around looking for us, yelling things like, "Skate fags!" "You're lame!" and "Cut your hair!" Sometimes they'd throw rocks and bottles at us.

Every skateboarder of my generation has experienced at least some of this. It was typical '80s jocks against skaters. It seemed like it was the five of us versus the entire rest of the school. This was especially hard for me because I had been one of the most popular guys in the group that was now putting me down—the same group that spit on me as I walked by.

People tell me that in a case as humiliating as being spit on, you should stand up for yourself no matter what the cost. That's what I call the "jail mentality": going toe-to-toe with someone who tests you, no matter what the consequence. To me, that idea stinks. People have been raised to think that there is some sort of honor in fighting. There are things worth fighting for, but pride isn't one of them. The easy thing to do would be to turn around and start swinging. What's really hard, and what really takes guts, is to keep

left: Joe and Christian checking out my ollie transfer at the Purple Ramp.

right on walking—confident in who you are and what you believe in. It didn't matter to me if some random jock didn't like how I looked. I wasn't out to prove anything to anyone. I was just being me. It was humiliating to be spit on, but there were some questions I had to ask myself. Would fighting the spitter erase my humiliation? Or would fighting him only give him what he was looking for? I am a firm believer in karma. I don't remember who the spitter was that day when I passed by my old "friends," but I believe that if he hasn't yet, he'll get his someday.

A Pro Board

Just off of our Boston skate loop was the Beacon Hill Skate Shop. One day when I was thirteen, I went in and got myself a complete board. I had saved up about a hundred bucks from odd jobs around the house, and I was helping my brother with his paper route by then. I picked out all the parts and had the guys at the shop put it together.

It was a Lance Mountain board by Powell. The Powell team was known as the "Bones Brigade"; the original members—including Lance Mountain, Tony Hawk, Mike McGill, and Steve Caballero—were my heroes. In the video I'd seen of them, it always looked like Lance was having the most fun, so I was stoked to ride his board. The board was the same fish shape that I liked and it had a white graphic with little black men running with surfboards under their arms. It had green Alva Rocks wheels and red Tracker Ultra-Light trucks.

Now I had my first pro model board, and I felt legit. It was so much more responsive. It turned better, had a stronger, stiffer deck, and would last twice as long as my old Variflex. I couldn't wait to get it home; it was going to be awesome.

above: Grant Brittain shot this self-portrait at the Nude Bowl, while I carved tiles above his head.

5.

melrose ramps

There were a lot of mistakes and some pretty bad ramps, but that's how we learned.

A while ago I got into a conversation with my mother about something that I probably shouldn't have. I told her how as a teenager with only a seventy-five cent weekly allowance, I was able to get all the wood needed to build our backyard ramps when we lived in Melrose. In the beginning my friends and I would beg and borrow any scraps we could find. The illegal stuff didn't happen until later. In the middle of this conversation I got the feeling that this was a story that my mother wasn't ready to hear.

Scrap Wood

We were all about thirteen years old when we started building small jump ramps that we would drag out into the street. The first ramps were nothing more than scrap wood leaned up against cinder blocks or bricks. It was even better when, in the winter, the snowplows would pile snow up along the street. Once the roads were cleared and dried by the sun, we'd lay some ply-wood on the snowbank and launch onto the sidewalk. You'd think snow would be bad for skateboarding, but in our case, we made the best of it. It was still freezing cold out, though. We'd wear lay-ers upon layers of sweatshirts, but we couldn't wear gloves because we needed to be able to grab our boards. For some rea-son, when you smack your hand down hard on the cement when you're freezing cold, it hurts twice as much.

Bigger and Better Ramps

As our skating skills improved the jump ramps got bigger and better. But now we needed more plywood, two-by-fours, a saw, and nails to build the kind of ramps we saw in magazines. No one ever showed us how to do it; we just looked at pictures and figured it out. Of course, there were a lot of mistakes and some pretty bad ramps, but that's how we learned.

I remember building one jump ramp that was four feet high with a pretty good kick to it. The plan was to use the ramp to jump over my mom's car. We got all our stuff together in my driveway and began building. We used my brother's jigsaw to cut all the wood. A jigsaw is meant for cutting small things like napkin holders in wood shop, but it was all we had. We were using it to cut some heavy-duty wood—and it wasn't easy.

When it came to surfacing the ramp, I learned a pretty painful lesson. We used only one layer of quarter-inch plywood, not knowing that we needed at least two. We dragged the ramp into the street and started sessioning. One minute I was blazing my sixth-grade method airs, and the next I was flying Superman-style over the back of the jump ramp without my board. At full speed my whole front truck had punched through the bottom of the ramp and stuck there. Not only did I learn a lesson about plywood, I learned something about skateboard-ing: One of the quirks that makes skateboarding different from other sports is the fact that taking a good slam (as long as you're not seriously hurt) is guaranteed to make your friends laugh hysterically.

Once we fixed the hole and added another layer, the ramp was good to go. We rolled my mother's Datsun station wagon backward down the driveway and into the street. Had any cars come by, it would have blocked traffic for sure. We dragged our new ramp up to the wagon and away we went. Mom never knew, but that day we were just like the guys in the magazines.

A Quarter Pipe in the Driveway

Eventually, my brother and I convinced my mom to let us build a quarter pipe at the end of our driveway near the street. We figured it would be about eight feet wide, and the driveway was about sixteen feet wide, so it shouldn't be a problem. Besides, it was a very long driveway, so a car could still enter, drive around the ramp, and park near the house. Of course, if we didn't swerve just right at the right time, the car was at risk for getting smashed. But we didn't let little details like that get in the way.

The timing for this project was perfect because our dad was visiting, and he kicked in to help buy the wood for the surface. He also helped us figure out the ramp plans that we had ordered from *Thrasher* magazine. We had been hammering boards together for so long without knowing what we were doing that it was amazing to see that there actually was a right way to do this!

This new ramp was big. It was eight feet wide and eight feet tall and had a deck at the top. It had eight-foot center radius transitions, so it went just up to vert. My brother and I and the other kids in the neighborhood spent hours doing laps up and down the driveway just working on our kickturns.

By the time this project was finished, our house looked like some kind of skatepark. We had the quarter pipe in the driveway and two or three jump ramps of different sizes lined up on the sidewalk. Looking back, at the time the neighbors must have thought we were nuts.

my first drop-in

My brother was a better skateboarder than I was when we built that quarter pipe. He went for the drop-in almost right away. As I remember, he made it with no problem. My first drop-in wasn't quite so successful.

The coping of the ramp was that aluminum threshold stuff that gets nailed down in a doorway to hold the carpet in place.

It was round in the front and good for grinds, but the back had a sharp lip on it. I was rocking a plastic tail skid on my Variflex board at the time, and as I went for the drop-in, the tail skid got caught on the lip of the coping and stuck. I slammed hard on my head and shoulder and got the wind knocked out of me. When I looked up, my board was still at the top of the ramp, hanging from that bent piece of coping.

A Home for Our Half Pipe

After just one New England winter our little quarter pipe was thrashed. It was rotted and warped and falling apart, so it was time to build another one. For this project there were more kids involved than just my brother and me. Kyle had moved on to high school and wasn't really skating as much anymore. So Jody, Christian, a couple other skaters from the neighborhood, and I started scrounging wood again in hopes of building a bigger, better quarter pipe. One of the kids had a father in the roofing business, so we had wood with roofing shingles and tar all over it. Another kid's dad was a cement contractor, and he'd give us the old plywood his company would use to make cement forms. We also would visit construction sites and lumberyards and ask for scrap wood. Eventually, we got to know the foremen at all the sites around town.

We had just finished building the frame for the new quarter pipe in my driveway when we got some unexpected great news. Our friend Billy Doyle, who was in my seventh-grade class, said his mother would let us build a half pipe in his backyard. Billy didn't even really skate, but that didn't bother us. We just wanted a place to put a half pipe. We had been begging our own parents for months with no luck. And now we had a chance to make our pipe dream a reality!

One day after school I rounded up a bunch of guys and told them the plan. We were going to carry the frame of our quarter pipe down to Billy's house, eleven blocks away. We were very serious and determined, but we must have looked ridiculous. One kid was in charge of running out into each intersection, watching for cars, and then giving us the go-ahead. About eight of us, all staggering under the weight of a half-built ramp, would then try to hurry

across the street and struggle down to the next block. Finally, we made it all the way to Billy's house and broke the picket fence as we handed the ramp over into to its new backyard home.

This was an ambitious project because we were talking about building another whole quarter pipe, plus a flat bottom and the two decks. That would require twice as much wood and work as anything we had ever faced. But we jumped into the project like we always did, without really worrying about how we would do it; we just knew that somehow we would make it work. And we did. The finished ramp was eight feet high and eight feet wide, with PVC pipe at the top, cut in half and nailed on for the coping. We built the whole thing with a few hammers and a hand-held jigsaw. Where we didn't have two-by-fours we used two-by-threes. Where we didn't have those, we just used thicker plywood to span the distance. The decks were four-by-eight sheets of three-quarter-inch plywood that had supports only around the edges. When you stood in the middle, the deck would sag a good three inches. Let's just say it wasn't quite built to code.

But it was great, and it was the first one like it in our town, and so word soon got around. Kids rode their bikes from neighboring towns to check it out. We would show up at the ramp, and there would be notes attached to it saying things like, *I'm Jimmy So-and-So from Saugus. Can I come back and ride this ramp sometime?* The more the merrier, we figured. All we wanted to do was skate, and it was great to have people to ride with.

Midnight Missions

Around this time all seven of us skaters in Melrose petitioned the city council to build a skateboard park. We dressed up nice and showed up at the council meetings. We presented our petitions and explained our plan, but we were simply too far ahead of our time. Or maybe Melrose was just too far behind the times. Today the city council there still hasn't approved a public skatepark, yet the skateboard population in Melrose has increased at least tenfold.

Anyway, frustrated with red tape and politics and tired of playing cat and mouse around town with police and security guards, we started taking matters into our own hands. By now

left: Frontside blunt in a backyard pool.

we had outgrown the ramp at Billy's house and wanted to go bigger. That's when we met Brent Carter. Brent was a BMX biker who had just built a ramp similar to ours way up on the other end of town. We decided to combine the wood from the two ramps and make a monster sixteen-foot-wide, nine-foot-high ramp. But that would take even more wood that we couldn't afford. Shut down by the city and desperate to progress, we resorted to stealing wood for our next project.

We decided to do our lumber liberating after dark, when everyone was asleep. Because Jody's parents were the most lenient of the lot, Jody's house became the preferred sleep-over locale. The easiest way to sneak out was from the sketchy fort we'd built in the rafters of Jody's garage. Basically, it was some plywood and rugs draped between crossbeams. Once during a sleep over, one of the support rigs gave out right under where I was sleeping. Luckily, my legs and hips fell first, and I managed to wake up and grab another two-by-four before I fell. Christian and Jody woke up just long enough to laugh at me.

Sneak-out sleep overs became missions. The plans had to be made beforehand so you knew what to pack. Regular sleep-over bags contained the usual: clothes, sleeping bags, the Missile Command game for the Atari, cards, and penny candy to trade. But a "mission bag" was very different. For this kind of sleep over I'd pack my McGyver kit, complete with Swiss army knife, sewing kit, matches, compass, and twine. I'd also throw in rope of different lengths and thicknesses, all black clothes, a black cap, and a flashlight. Usually around one or two in the morning, when we were sure Jody's parents were asleep, it was mission time. Christian taught us how to burn a cork and paint our faces black. Once our faces were painted, we'd go down the fire pole to the garage floor, out the side window, and through Mrs. Adams's yard to freedom. (Jody always seemed more afraid of getting caught by Mrs. Adams than by his mother. I never did ask why.)

Each mission route was carefully planned in advance. We weren't sneaking out to fool around—we knew exactly what we were going to do. On one night, for instance, we might go to pick up the three sheets of plywood that we knew were left at the

Kick flip melon onto the hip of the Combi-Bowl
in Orange, California.

© Brittain

right: Tuck knee invert at Brent Carter's ramp in Melrose. Check the style: thrift-store plaid shorts over cutoff striped pajamas.

bottom left: Cooling down in Chicago under a sprinkler with my first board (Powell, Lance Mountain) and my original bucket cap.

bottom right: Every day on vacation in Flagler Beach, Florida, my pop would buy my brother and me two Dr. Peppers and a box of Cracker Jacks for the beach. We thought we were the luckiest kids in the world.

© Steve Shea

above: Frontside stalefish at Escondido.

right: My dad shot this photo of Kyle and me while camping on Lake Huron in Canada. I remember not liking it when I was younger because it showed my brother jumping higher than me.

I convinced the Ocean Beach Park to let me skate late one night—
one of the perks of being a pro skater.

clockwise from top left: My 5th
birthday party in Ann Arbor, Michigan;
Tony Hawk and I after our F-18 flight;
Family portrait.

© Britain

above: Look, Mom, no hands!

above: Chillin' with Run-DMC in Long Beach, California.

right: Chris "Rhino" Rooney: friend, photographer, skater. Backside two-out in a backyard pool.

© Wez Lundry

Frontside lien 540 over the channel at Encinitas.

© RHINO

new house they were building on Vinton Street. On another night we might head straight to the stack of two-by-fours left behind Ceritani's market, where they were doing some remodeling.

We were very serious about our missions at the time, but looking back on them now, I have to ask: What were we thinking!? Picture looking out your window at night and seeing three fifteen-year-old kids running up the street, dressed all in black, with black smeared all over their faces, looking like some kind of commando burglars. Now picture each of these kids carrying a four-by-eight-foot sheet of heavy three-quarter-inch plywood on his back. It got even more ridiculous if someone yelled, "Car!" Then we'd all drop our plywood and dive into the nearest bushes. We'd do this over and over until we finally made it back to Jody's house, where we'd add our loot to the growing woodpile behind the garage. We stored the wood there until Jody's parents went out for dinner or something, leaving their station wagon at home. Then Jody, only fifteen and without a license, would drive the load of wood up to Brent's house. Mission accomplished.

All for a Cause

I felt bad when I told my mom that we used to steal wood, because she looked so disappointed. I guess I just figured that after all these years she would have figured it out. It takes hundreds of two-by-fours to build a ramp, and the cheapest wood you could get at the time was maybe a dollar a stud. As I said, I used to get seventy-five cents per week for allowance if I did all my chores. You do the math.

Before or since those days I never stole as much as a candy bar from a convenience store. But in those years we sure stole a lot of lumber. Looking back, I know it was wrong, but I guess I rationalized it—and at the time I felt justified in doing what we had to do to have a place to skate. None of our parents had come through with a place or the money to build a ramp (not that they could have afforded it, anyway). The city had turned us down on a public park and chased us away from every good spot around town—yet there were public basketball and tennis courts on every corner. Had we not stolen the wood to build our ramps, I might not have become what I am today.

The Purple Ramp

The last big ramp built in my Melrose era was the "Purple Ramp." Jody's parents had finally given in to the pressures of their sons (Jody's brother, Matt, had become a skater now too). They gave us the okay to build our biggest ramp yet in their yard. It was a seven-foot-tall, twenty-foot-wide miniramp. On one of the decks was a "Chin Ramp"—style two-foot-high, eight-foot-wide microramp. To us, it was just like the ramp the Bones Brigade rode.

Our ramp-building skills had come a long way, as had our covert wood-collecting abilities. The ramp had steel coping, "borrowed" from a fence we'd taken apart down by the train tracks, and we even had a circular saw to cut the two-by-fours. By this time some of the skaters in the area were old enough to have jobs and drive. We took collections, and after everyone chipped in, we were able to buy the top layer of plywood. Jody and I collected leftover house paint from our basements, of all different colors and all different types—indoor, outdoor, glossy, and flat, it didn't matter. When we mixed it all together, it was a bright purple. Thus the legendary Purple Ramp.

I got to skate that ramp for only one spring because I spent my summers in Michigan with my dad. But we had some great sessions there, and I learned some cool miniramp tricks, including ollie grabs and ollie blunts. The sweetest part was the microramp on the deck. You could fly out of the seven foot and land to tail or grind and then transfer back.

Unfortunately, the Purple Ramp was not up for even a year before neighbors complained about the noise and got after Jody's parents about zoning laws. Jody's father was a lawyer, but even that didn't help. After a short legal battle and yet another plea for a public skateboard park, we were forced to take it down. Once again I was feeling cheated by my town. The city of Ann Arbor, Michigan, where I spent my summers, had just built a public skate ramp. Why not Melrose? Most frustrating of all, less than a year after the Purple Ramp was gone, the complaining neighbors moved away. The majority of the wood was scrapped, but we saved some and later built another microramp inside Jody's two-car garage.

right: Big 540 at Encinitas.

© RHINO

Lucky for me, around the time the Purple Ramp came down, a little skate shop in Cambridge acquired some warehouse space and was building what would become the second-longest-running indoor skatepark in the country. It was the first skatepark the Boston area had seen since Shooting Star closed in the late '70s. The place was named Z.T. Maximus, and it was to become my second home.

Looking Back

Skating had taught me and my friends all about learning by trial and error. If something doesn't work, you either try again or try something else. That lesson definitely carried over to building our ramps. We learned from our mistakes, and sometimes we got lucky and got it right on the first try. Just like in skateboarding, there was no coach or adult telling us the "right" way to do it and we did it all ourselves. I admit that there were times when it was hard to get kids to stop skating long enough to hammer some nails. We all would have been happier skating, and the money we used to buy wood came from the little we had saved to buy a new skateboard or a set of wheels. But we were willing to make some sacrifices and motivate one another to make our dream take shape.

Every so often adults would come by the ramp to check it out. They always seemed so amazed by what we'd built all by ourselves, and I never quite understood their surprise. Looking back now, I can see that what we did was pretty awesome. Skateboarders in my parents' generation might not have done more than nail their old roller-skate wheels to a two-by-four to make a scooter. But because of what I lived through growing up as a skateboarder, I'm not surprised by what I see young skaters achieve these days. Kids are capable of wonderful and amazing things all by themselves—all adults have to do is stand back and let them try.

6.

thank god for skateparks
"I'm going to be coming here a lot."

When I was a kid, the only good place to skate in the winter was on our homemade ramps after we shoveled off the snow. But when I was fourteen, all that changed when indoor skateparks began to open in the Boston area.

Maximus

Z.T. Maximus was the first park to open. It was in an old warehouse next to the city projects, right around the corner from the C-Bowl in Cambridge. It wasn't the best part of town but it was the best thing I had seen up to that point in my life. Jody, Christian, and I went over to see the place when it was being built, and we couldn't believe it.

The biggest, gnarliest, widest vert ramp we had ever built was sixteen feet wide, nine feet high, and made of old scrap wood. This was brand new and built by professional ramp builders. It was twenty-four feet wide and nine feet high, plus there was a sixteen-foot-wide miniramp behind it. Because the ceilings were low (about fifteen feet), you could stand on the deck of the big ramp and hold on to the rafters. Obviously, you couldn't go very high, but I wasn't blasting big airs anyway.

"How About Some Skate Bucks?"

Whenever the weather was bad, I'd go straight from school to Z.T. Maximus. I would skate a mile over to the train station, do my homework during the hour-long train ride, and skate all afternoon. That was my life.

At first I worried that this routine would get too expensive. There was no way I could afford to pay to skate every day. So I introduced myself to Zito (otherwise known as Ken Deutsche) who ran the shop, hoping that once he got to know me, he'd let me skate for free.

"I'm going to be coming here a lot," I told him.

Zito looked at me and smiled.

"I'm going to come almost every day," I persisted.

"Right on," he said, walking away. And that was the end of it.

But I wasn't discouraged; I'd just have to keep trying.

It wasn't long before Zito saw that I really was serious about skateboarding. He then became what I'd call my first "sponsor"; he let me skate for free. Of course, Zito needed some money to keep the place going, so once in a while he'd skate over with his hand out saying, "Hey, kids, how 'bout some skate bucks?" and we'd all give him a couple dollars. But he was always very generous to the locals.

Hanging with Older Guys

Some of the guys who skated Z.T.'s became my mentors. Frank the Wrecka' (outside of Boston he'd be the Wrecker) and Jeff the Alien (formerly called "Fingers" because once in a skate collision he ran over a guy's hand and ruined his fingers) were the heroes of the skateboard scene in Boston at that time. They were in their twenties (which seemed old to me) and had been skating way before my time. They were great skaters who were getting airs out of the Cambridge pool when I could just barely get grinds. They were ripping the Maximus vert ramp when I was just learning.

I remember the day I met one of the best: Kevin Day. He had a board sponsor and a clothing sponsor so he was big time for Boston back then, but I had never seen him. One of my first times at Maximus I was standing on the deck, and I said to this guy who was skating with me, "Hey, you're rippin.' Do you skate the Cambridge pool?" Kevin knew right away that I didn't know who he was, and he just smiled while I kept at it. "Do you skate with Kevin Day and those guys?" He still kept smiling and finally said, "I *am* Kevin Day." Wow! I began babbling: "Cool! Right on! Nice to meet you!" Kevin just laughed and rolled over to drop in as I stood there staring. Eventually, as I got better, we skated together and actually helped each other. I taught Kevin some newer tricks, like mute-grab blunt 180s, and he taught me the standards, like frontside inverts.

big time

In my freshman year of high school a production company came to Maximus looking for a skater to cast in a Marshmallow Fluff TV ad, and I got the lead. Fluff is a very East Coast thing. It's basically whipped-up marshmallows that you spread on bread with peanut butter to make a "Fluffernutter" sandwich. It sounds gross, but it's really good. Health-nut Mom would never get it for us, but I used to trade stuff with other kids in the lunchroom for a Fluffernutter on white every once in a while.

The story line of the thirty-second spot was about a kid (me) sitting in class looking bummed and impatient. When the school bell rings, all the kids jump up and run out of the room. It breaks to a scene of me running out the front door of the school with all the kids following me. I boneless down the stairs and start skating home. The kids keep following me through a park (called "Turtles") that has sloping, curving cement banks everywhere, creating natural jump ramps. I do a trick on the bank; I do a handstand and carve across the Fluff sign and then do a 360 off a jump ramp. By the time I get home there are tons of kids following me on foot, on bikes, and on roller skates. My "mom" greets us at the door and invites everyone in for Fluffernutter sandwiches.

Although it was a little tiring doing the scenes over and over again, with the director saying things like, "Smile more this time" and "Remember how excited you are to see that plate of Fluffernutters," it was a great experience. When the commercial aired, kids in school would recognize me and say, "Hey, you're the Fluffernutter kid!" Being recognized like that gave me a hint of what was to come.

Secondhand Smoke

After Maximus opened, other parks followed. As I got to know the older skaters better they began to take me with them. One of our favorite parks was The Playground in Wallingford, Connecticut. I'd meet the guys at Maximus or at the Forest Hills stop at the end of the Orange train line, and we'd all pile into the designated "skate mobile." I figured I was the luckiest skater on the East Coast to be hanging out with these guys.

The only thing was that they were all stoners. They smoked pot no matter where we went. Almost every time, I'd find myself alone in the middle of a skate session because they were all taking a smoke break out in the van. One time during the two-hour ride to The Playground they were blazing joints the whole time. I never had any interest in smoking, so I just stayed out of it.

When we got to Connecticut, I put on my pads, took three runs, and just knew I wasn't feeling it. On the fourth run I locked up on an alley-oop backside air and slammed on my head. That took me out for the day, and I was so mad—especially when I realized it happened because I got a contact high from all the smoke in the van. Now I had to sit around and wait for them to finish skating before the two-hour ride back home.

Because I looked up to these guys, I guess it's surprising that I didn't take my turn when joints were passed to me. But outside of some good-natured ribbing, they never pushed me to smoke or drink. I'd just pass it on and that was it. It never occurred to me that I should get high, because all I wanted was to skate my best, and I knew pot wasn't going to help. All I thought about was learning new stuff and getting better. Slamming on my head and missing out on a whole day of skating reaffirmed why I didn't want to smoke dope.

On the Road

I got my own driver's license when I was sixteen and a half. Not wanting to waste any time, the day I got my license I convinced my mom to not only let me borrow the car, but also to let me drive on the freeway for the first time. I picked up Jody, Christian, and our two friends from Saugus, Chuck and Derek. We were so psyched as we started the hour-long trip down to the Skate Hut in Providence, Rhode Island.

It wasn't an easy trip. We were cruising along for almost an hour when I asked Jody to grab the directions off the dashboard and tell me where to exit. As he reached for the paper he rolled down his window, and the directions blew right out of the car. Now we had no idea how to find the skatepark. We got off in Providence and drove around some pretty sketchy areas, asking people if they knew where the Skate Hut was. No one had any idea. After a long time Jody saw a car pass by that had skate stickers on it. "Follow that car!" he yelled. We tailed the car for about two miles and landed right in front of the Skate Hut, just like we planned.

The Skate Hut was even better than Maximus. It was in a huge brick building that was an abandoned electrical plant. The vert ramp was built wall to wall, and compared to the vert ramp at Maximus, it was huge. There was twenty-five feet of ceiling space (versus the fifteen feet at Maximus), and the ramp was twenty-four feet wide, with nine-foot transitions and two feet of vert. On one side it had cement pool coping rather than steel pipe. The Skate Hut also had a spine miniramp and the "cheese ramp" (a two-foot-high microramp).

Fred Smith, a pro for Alva at the time, had started the park with a few friends. He and his buddies lived in rooms they put together right in the skatepark. They were always there and always good to me.

The Nickname Game

Throughout the skateboard world you'll find that most skaters have or have had nicknames—whether they like it or not. Sometimes the false names stick, and people are known only by their aliases. Lots of times the alias comes from a shortened

Kick flip melon over the ladder at the Gonzales pool in Los Angeles, California.

© RHINO

version of someone's first or last name. Steve Rouge, the former head judge of World Cup Skateboarding, for example, has always been known as "Shrewgy." One of the best pool skaters in the world is known by most as "Salba" (Steve Alba). He's got a brother named "Malba" (Mickey Alba). My teammate on Powell, Steve Caballero, is simply called "Cab."

Among Boston skaters like Kevin Day, Frank the Wrecka, and Jeff the Alien, I was called "Wonder Boy." Fred Smith gave me the name at the Skate Hut because I would learn a new trick on almost every visit to the park. One day I walked in and Fred said, "What's up, Wonder Boy?" and it stuck.

Here's the inside story on a few crazy names:

- "TYCO"—Sean Flemming is only about 4 feet 11 inches tall but he skates pools so fast that he resembles a Tyco race set slot car.
- "BABY JESUS"—Sergie Ventura was said to be the protégé of the legendary Christian Hosoi (inventor of the Christ air). These days Christian is simply known as "Holmes."
- "SIX TOES"—Colixto Hernandez was named in a case of pure laziness. *Six Toes* just turned out to be easier to say than *Colixto.*
- "540"—Mark Hayes got his name because he used to be the master of 540 slides. He's a bit on the chunky side these days, so people like to kid him about his name being simply a description of his weight. His mom once suggested that the numbers had just been mixed up—that his nickname had really come from his batting average in maintaining a steady girlfriend: 0 for 5.

There are also skateboarders nicknamed "Zizza," "Rhino," "Bacon," "Muscles," "Loaf," "Sweat Neck," "Bird Man," "Morty," "The Package," "Moses," "G-man," "Roach," "Vertical Vampire," "Holmes," "Pee-Wee," "Mad Dog," "Ruler," "Spiderman," "The Jedi," "Cookie Head," "Twister," "Pit Bull," and "The Gonz." There's always a good story behind how each skater got his name.

Skating Ratz

When I was a junior in high school, a park named Ratz opened in the sticks of Maine in a tiny little town called Biddeford. The building was built specifically to be a skateboard park rather than being a converted warehouse, like most other indoor parks. There was plenty of ceiling space, and the concrete floor was poured on two separate levels. The vert ramp was built on the lower level to give more headroom. It was forty feet wide, with nine-foot transitions and two feet of vert. This was the biggest, best, smoothest, and by far the widest vert ramp I had ever skated. Ratz also had a wooden bowl that was ten feet and eight feet deep in different sections. There was a spine ramp and a street course. It was a legit park when it first opened. You actually paid when you walked in and then got one of those little wristbands.

It was a two-hour drive to Ratz, so I couldn't go there after school, but I'd often head up there on Saturdays or Sundays. If I couldn't get the car, I could still bum rides off my friends. One of the more memorable rides was with Kevin Day. He had just bought a brand-new van. Kevin had read in the driver's manual that he shouldn't drive the new engine over fifty-five miles an hour for the first couple hundred miles or so. And he wasn't going to break the rule. We were driving in the middle lane on the Maine Turnpike, poking along with cars passing us on either side. We were so bummed, we were all complaining: "Come on, Grandma! I want to get some skating time in today before the park closes!" Then I looked out the window and couldn't believe what I saw. There were four nuns, black-and-white habits and all, passing us on the right in a Volkswagen Beetle! Kevin never heard the end of that one.

Sponsored!

When I was sixteen, a guy named Jeff walked up to me at the Skate Hut and handed me some business cards and T-shirts from a clothing company called Jobless. (Jobless sponsored Kevin Day and so I guess he told them about me.) "Hey," he said, "call me sometime and I'll send you more clothing." Before that day I had never thought I was good enough to be sponsored. I certainly wasn't looking for sponsorship, and I didn't even really understand the whole concept.

Soon after that, another guy from a company called Flight gave me a T-shirt and said, "Call me and I'll send you some boards." That sounded really good. I called, and he sent me two boards worth about fifty bucks each. I couldn't believe it. Free boards! I gave one to my brother and kept one. All I had to do was wear the T-shirt and use the board in any contests I entered. So now I was sponsored.

Although putting on a T-shirt and being sponsored seemed so easy, it really changed everything. The skateboard contests I entered at this time were put together by local skate shops. They had divisions for novice, intermediate, advanced, and sponsored skaters. I had always entered the advanced division, but now I had to step up and compete against the big guns like Kevin Day. By now I knew I wanted to be a pro skateboarder one day, and this was the next step in that direction.

My sponsored status and my dreams of going pro accompanied me that summer when I went to visit my dad in Michigan. It was just the start of great things to come.

7.
skating michigan
"You can do it!"

It's not that I ever wanted my parents to be divorced, but there was an upside to the situation. I was lucky because I could skate the New England area by my mom in the winter and then skate Michigan all summer with my dad cheering me on.

Dropping in on a Half Pipe
In the summer of 1986 I turned thirteen and was going into seventh grade. I landed in Michigan with my Variflex board under my arm, ready to find a good place to skate. Right away my dad brought my brother and me to a local skateboard shop.

We were looking around when a shaggy-looking teenage kid came in. My dad completely embarrassed us by going up to him and saying, "I want you to meet my boys, who just got into skating." And he wasn't finished. "Do you know any good places to skate around here?" he asked. A little taken aback at first, the kid was totally cool and gave us his phone number and said he'd take us around and introduce us to other skaters in the area. This kid, Dave Tuck, became a good friend of ours.

Dave was a few years older than Kyle, and he had his own car. He picked us up the next day and brought us to Jeff Hadley's house in a town called Ypsilanti. Hadley had built a half pipe vert ramp in his backyard that he let the local guys use. It was sixteen feet wide and eleven feet high; it had plastic coping on top and was painted two different shades of pink. It was beautiful. At this point I had been riding the quarter pipe at home in our driveway, but we had not yet built the other ramps and I had not yet dropped in on a half pipe. Kyle dropped in on the pink pipe almost right away, but I still wasn't ready. So I just fakied back and forth most of that summer.

But the next summer before eighth grade I was ready—or at least Dave kept telling me I was. With my dad nearby with his video camera, I stood on the deck of Hadley's ramp looking down from eleven feet up, scared to death.

"Go ahead!" yelled Dave. "You can do it!"

"Don't think about it," added my dad. "Just do it."

Taking a big breath, I dropped in—actually, smashed in is more like it. I stepped too far forward on the nose of my board and went right over. I slammed on my elbow and ribs, knocking the wind out of myself.

"Okay, try again," said my dad from behind the video camera. My dad wasn't one to panic over a fall. He just kept right on recording. I looked back up at the top of the ramp. Eleven feet is almost the height of a one-story building. But if my brother could do it, so could I. I climbed back up, took another deep breath, and dropped in. This time I made it! Everyone yelled for me, and I ran back up the ramp to do it again. It was definitely the highlight of my summer. After that I could drop in on any half pipe I skated.

The AKR Tour

By the summer of '89, when I was sixteen, summers in Michigan were really busy. In between my work hours serving up food at Red Hot Lovers (a hot-dog joint), I spent most of my time skating. Every day I skated the steel, city vert ramp that was thirty-two feet wide and eleven feet high, with a roll-in channel and two extensions. (The steel would get so hot that once we cooked hot dogs on it!) There was also some good pool skating in the area at abandoned hotels. And there was an indoor park called the Skate Escape. But I wanted more.

My pop suggested we take a road trip down the East Coast. So we piled into his new used minivan and the Andy/Kyle/Rod (AKR) tour officially began. I even made T-shirts for each of us with *AKR Tour 19SK-89* on them, and my dad brought his trusty video camera along. We went on the road for two weeks, mapping a route according to skate spots and campgrounds. We'd stop at night and set up our tent at campgrounds, or else we'd stay with skaters who were kind enough to offer their couches and floors to sleep on. It was the best vacation in the world.

We worked our way down through Pennsylvania and to the Ocean Bowl Skatepark in Maryland. Once we were on the coast, my dad called ahead and found out that the park in North Carolina was going to be closed on the one day we would be there. Without hesitation, he called the local newspaper and told a reporter our story.

"I'm making a film of the AKR East Coast Tour with amateur skateboarders," he said with a straight face. "Can you get the owner of the local skatepark to open up on Monday for us?"

The next thing you know, we pull up to the park and the owner rushes out to greet us. While my dad "interviewed" him on video about the history of the park, Kyle and I had the whole place to ourselves. You gotta love my dad.

Then we went on to skate the "farm ramp" in South Carolina. It was actually two ramps placed side by side. It was about one hundred feet wide, which made it the biggest ramp in existence at that time. There were two hips and a three-quarter pipe at one end. My brother thrust big frontsides into the three-quarter pipe, and I learned slob fast plants over the channel. It was a dream ramp and a big stop on the tour.

Our next stop was Florida. We had planned to hit three different parks during our four-day stay there, but then plans changed. We went to a brand-new park in Daytona Beach called

right: Frontside blunt on the Bird Perch in Encinitas, California.

Stone Edge that was all cement bowls. We had so much fun the first day that we decided to skate that park for all three days!

When it was time to head back home, we drove north to the Cedar Crest Country Club in Virginia; it was our last stop on the tour. They had a huge steel ramp and a camping ground right next to it. It was a perfect setup for us, but it turned out to be not quite a perfect day for me. This ramp is where I took one of the nastiest slams of my career.

The ramp was thirty-two feet wide, and it had a channel in it where, instead of having the vert and the coping, there was a roll-in that left a gap you had to air over. I had skated channels before but this one had only eight feet of ramp on the other side of it. Being the beginner that I was, I did an air over the channel and got the wobbles as I landed. As I came across the flat bottom heading toward the edge of the ramp, I had to decide whether to slam against the other wall or jump off the side of the ramp. I decided too late and was almost halfway up the wall before I bailed off the side. I shot my board straight into the air while I went flying off to the right. I straddled a picnic table on my way to the ground and thought for sure I had broken my upper leg. As I lay curled in pain my board came back down like a missile and hit me on the top of the head. I was rolling around swearing my head off, but fortunately, I was all in one piece. And good ol' Dad got the whole thing on tape. We definitely could have sent that one to *America's Funniest Home Videos*. In fact, when I was on *The Tonight Show* in 2001, Jay Leno showed that video. It was still good for a laugh.

dear concerned father

Skateboarding is not like the sports most parents were raised with, and sometimes it scares them. Here's a letter I received from a worried dad after I turned pro. I think my reply will explain why I believe skateboarding is good for kids, even when parents don't understand.

Dear Andy Macdonald's Management,

I am a father of 8- and 10-year-old boys. We are a middle-class family and reside in a fairly affluent suburb. Both my boys are very interested in skateboarding. Fundamentally I see no problems with the sport of skate-

boarding. I do have a major concern about the negative subculture that exists in the sport. For example, I have had a hard time finding any skateboarding videos that are not laced with f-bombers and other offensive language. Many skateboarders I have observed on TV, in videos, and in or around our town have an image of blatant disrespect for the law.

Our local skate shop resembles a head shop or tattoo parlor. In addition, the music associated with skating is often violent in nature and laced with offensive language. As much as I like the sport of skateboarding, I see the sport as a negative influence on our youth. My concern is great enough that my wife and I may intentionally try to stop their interest in the sport. Do you have any ideas of how I can guide my boys to the positive side of skating?

Sincerely,

Concerned Father

Dear Concerned Father,

From your letter, I gather that you understand and appreciate skateboarding as a sport. However, I feel you are greatly underestimating its potential. By the time I had entered the sixth grade, I was participating in just about every team sport you can think of. By my second year of skateboarding I had dismissed all my team sports as too rigid, boring, and time-consuming. I became a skateboarder. In skating there was no coach to tell me when to practice. I had to be more dedicated and put in more effort than I had in any of the sports I had given up. I learned lessons in self-motivation and self-determination that still hold fast today. These qualities are the essence and core of the subculture that concerns you.

I believe that the negative aspects of skateboarding are disproportionately highlighted because of the sport's tender age, along with the subsequent ignorance that skateboarding even exists on a professional level. From my perspective, mainstream sports are historically every bit as, if not more, subversive, violent, and "laced with offensive language." Fighting is not only permitted, but often encouraged, in hockey. Babe Ruth, a hero of baseball, was known to be a womanizer and a drinker. The World Series was fixed and Pete Rose seemed to have turned out as many bets as he did hits. I won't even go into the NFL, but suffice it to say that what you might see in skateboarding videos pales in comparison to the criminal record of just one NFL team today.

Why are skateboarders seen as disrespectful of the law? Because skateboarding is outlawed in almost every metropolitan area. Yet, in most cases, they are the only places to skateboard. Try to imagine what it might *be like to be yelled at, to have your equipment confiscated, to be chased away, fined, or even imprisoned every time you went out to practice your sport. It's really no wonder that many skateboarders are on the defensive. Think of what a mess there would be if, all of a sudden, there were no public places to practice football or baseball or soccer. We wouldn't expect people to just stop participating in those sports. It's even possible that they might take to the streets, as skateboarders have been forced to do.*

As for your concern about music, all different skaters listen to all different types of music. When I was your sons' age, I listened almost exclusively to reggae music, influenced by the older kids I skated with. The majority of reggae singers speak about smoking marijuana because it's a large part of the Rastafarian religion. But I was far too busy skateboarding to be concerned with the lyrics of the music I was skating to. To this day I have never taken as much as a drag from a cigarette, never mind tried drugs of any kind. Your children's decisions as to whether or not they will try drugs or speak certain words will go far beyond the messages they hear in music or skate videos.

As for the decor of skate shops, my local skate shop looks like The Gap and I don't like it. The point is: If you don't like the way your local skate shop presents skateboarding, don't patronize it. I'm sure there are other skate shops in your area, and if not, you can order equipment through mail-order catalogs.

So is skateboarding a negative influence on our youth? My answer is no, plain and simple. The lessons of self-motivation and discipline in this coachless sport make it worth a try. It was the most creative, self-fulfilling, and confidence-boosting outlet that I found at your children's age. Skateboarding is what I do for a living now. Financially, I am doing well because of it. I've traveled all over the world and witnessed a brotherhood that you will not find in any other sport. I am a spokesperson for the Partnership for a Drug-Free America, as well as for Board Aid (an organization that raises money and awareness for teens with AIDS). I am on the board of directors at the YMCA to help with youth programs, and I am a community activist in pursuit of public skateboard parks. Most importantly, I am a skateboarder. Don't let your kids miss out.

Sincerely,

Andy Macdonald

NSA

I kept skating and learning new tricks throughout the winters in Boston and the summers in Michigan. In the summer of 1990, just before my junior year of high school, I felt I was ready to enter my first National Skateboard Association (NSA) competition. The district qualifiers for my area in Michigan were held five hours away in Rockford, Illinois. Everybody there was the best of the best. I remember seeing Darren Navarette, Brian Patch, and Eric Koston, who are all pro skaters today. I entered only the vert that year, not expecting to even qualify. I worked on my line over and over during the practice sessions, trying to decide if I should do the 360 varials I had just learned. Sometimes they worked; sometimes they didn't. In the end, I wimped out and cut them from my line. I also worked on my Christ air to fakie during practice (which makes you look like Christ, with your feet off the board, both legs straight down, and both arms straight out), but when my back foot missed the tail one time, I slammed so hard on the metal ramp that I thought I was going to pass out; I decided to leave that out too.

I don't remember the whole line, but whatever I did, it was good enough to get me fifth place in my first NSA vert contest. (Dave LaRue won with a score that was five points higher than everybody else's.) Now I had to figure out how to get down to the regionals in Springfield, Missouri. One way or the other, I was on my way!

Three weeks later, with a board from my Flight sponsor and $50 from my clothing sponsor, Jobless, I grabbed a ride with other skaters going to Springfield, which was a sixteen-hour car ride away. We got there okay and even found the skatepark no problem.

Sarge, the team guy for G&S, let me mooch some floor space in the hotel room for the weekend. And I did okay in the contest, but I didn't qualify in the top ten, so I wasn't eligible for the finals. I remember thinking that it didn't seem fair that three of the five judges were from Texas and nine of the top ten qualifiers were from Texas. (A dozen years later skateboard competitions are still plagued by politics and claims of biased judging.) But that's just the way things were, and I probably wasn't ready for the finals yet anyway. I headed back to Michigan with lots of memories and lessons learned about skating in the big leagues.

The Finals

The following summer in '91, I got another chance. That summer didn't start out so great—my dad had divorced "Sharon #1" and

moved in with "Sharon #2" in Lansing, Michigan. I didn't like Lansing as much as Ann Arbor for skating, but now that I was going into my senior year of high school, I knew it would be my last summer in Michigan. I made the best of it, and it wasn't so bad.

I qualified in the NSA district competitions in both vert and miniramp. I again headed to Springfield for the regionals with my friend Dave Campbell. I had my license at this point, so we shared the driving, and I arrived once again with little money but very high hopes. We rolled into town late at night and had enough money for only one night's hotel stay. After skating practice the next day we had no place to go, but we had a plan.

We hung around waiting for people to start leaving the bars, and we both started juggling on a street corner. Dave was the real showman and looked the part. He was balding but he had dreadlocks halfway down his back and a big puffy "neck beard." He would skate with a skirt over his skate shorts. (The other skaters had dubbed him the "skating Amish man.") I showed off with my diablo and my devil sticks while Dave juggled balls. We passed six clubs for our finale. Dave handed around his knit Rasta hat at the end for tips. Surprisingly, we made enough money for a hotel that night and the entry fee the next day. Even though I hardly got any sleep, everything went right for me the next day. I qualified for the finals in both miniramp and vert and headed home a stoked little dude.

Now I had to get ready for my trip to the finals in Atlanta, Georgia. We decided to make it a big family affair. My brother, who had been working in Germany for the summer, flew back to see me. Mom flew in from Massachusetts, while Pop, Sharon, and I made the two-day drive from Michigan. Obviously, the NSA National Finals were a big deal to all of us. It was a contest among the top ten riders in each of the three regional contests— West Coast, East Coast, and Central. If you placed in the top five, you'd probably go pro within the next year. In fact, if you look at the roster of those top thirty skaters, you'll see that about eighty percent of them are the top pros today: street skaters like Eric Koston, Willy Santos, Chris Senn, Wade Spire, and Fred Gall; and vert skaters like Colin McKay, Brian Howard, and me.

right: Air Andy.

The contest was held in an indoor park called the Skate Zone. It had a wooden bowl that I had seen in magazines and couldn't wait to skate. Even though it was a million degrees in Atlanta, my brother and I spent hours sessioning the bowl when I should have been practicing for the contest. I did my tricks just fine, but I still placed somewhere in the teens: I did a fakie 540 over the hip and a one-footed frontside grind on the miniramp. I also did a trick I made up called the "mummy." It's a body wrap lien to tail; you ride up frontside, pass the board around your body behind your back, put it back on your feet, then smack the tail and come in. Of course I had hoped to do better, but I did place sixth in miniramp. I was so stoked to be there that I didn't feel let down at all.

I even got a mention in *Transworld Skateboarding* magazine. They said something about Andy Macdonald doing tricks no one had ever seen before. That's when I realized how out of it I really was. I just made up my own tricks because I didn't know about the "cool" tricks they were doing out in California. All I knew or cared about was that I wanted to be a professional skateboarder. By making it to the finals that summer, I had gotten one step closer to my goal.

8.
senior year
They gave me gym credit for skateboarding!

One of the best things about going to school was being with my friends. Because most of my friends were a year older than I was, I wasn't looking forward to my senior year at Melrose High without them. Just when I was getting down about it at the end of my junior year, I was given a surprise choice.

"Andy," my mother said one night, "I want to move to Newton to live with my boyfriend, Michael. Do you want me to wait until after you graduate high school next year? Or would you like to transfer to the high school in Newton and move with me now?"

Even though I wasn't happy at Melrose, this wasn't an easy decision. I found out in second grade that it isn't fun to be the new kid in town. But when I added up the pros and cons, there was far more good stuff about moving this time than bad: Newton North High was a great school; I already knew some kids from there through my church in Boston; there was nothing at Melrose left for me; and the move would make my mom happy. I also figured that I had only one year left before I moved to California to become a pro skateboarder, so what difference did it really make? I decided that when I returned from my summer in Michigan with my dad, I'd move to Newton and start all over again. This turned out to be the best decision of my life.

Fitting Right In

The house we rented in Newton was only four blocks from the high school, so I skated over on my first day and saw immediately that Newton was no Melrose. There was an outdoor area called "the mall" that had a stage and stairs where kids were skateboarding! In the front of the school there were slanted walls that were perfect for wallriding, and no adults were around saying, *You can't skate here!* The school itself was much more open and liberal, more like a college campus. If I had a class, I went to it; but if I didn't have a class, I could go home, get something to eat, and come back later. I didn't need hall passes, and it didn't feel like a prison. And most surprising to me, the football players didn't rule, and nobody was put down for looking different.

Right away I met the school's skaters—we were hard to miss, wearing our skate logo T-shirts and thrashed Airwalks. It was so easy: "Hey, dude, you skate?" and new friendships began. I also met lots of kids who weren't skaters, but who were just good people and welcomed me without hesitation. One guy was Dan Worth, who knew a good friend of mine, Liz Chang, from my church youth group. On my first day of school he came right up to me and said, "Hey, you're Andy Macdonald, right?" Because Dan was down with a lot of popular kids in school, right away I was too. How could I ever have thought twice about coming here? Change is good.

Skating for Gym Credit

I knew this was going to be a good year—and it quickly got better. In this new high school they gave me gym credit for skateboarding! In a program called "Contract Gym," students could get credit for extracurricular physical activities and then skip gym class. I had to sign a contract that promised that I would skateboard at least two times a week (no problem for me), and it had to be signed by an adult supervisor. As far as Newton North High School knew, Ken Deutsche at Z.T. Maximus was my coach. He had to sign these little slips of paper that I handed in to my gym teacher every week. My friend Mark had Contract Gym too, so we'd go to the park together pretty much every night.

Even the class scheduling at Newton North was great for me. Because I knew I wasn't going to college (even though my mother was still hoping), I took the fewest number of credits I needed to graduate. I was finished with my classes before noon, which gave me plenty of time to go home, cook up some macaroni and cheese, and squeeze in some skating before going to work at a local video store (I was saving up money for my move to California). Life doesn't get better than this when you're in high school.

My Future Wife

When March rolled around, I was making plans to spend my spring break in California. This would be my first time back since I visited Disneyland with my father when I was eight. Although my mother was sure I would never really go, I already had my plane ticket and had lined up some youth hostels to stay at. This was the trip that would help me decide if I really wanted to move there and try to become a pro skater.

All I could think about was California. I daydreamed about it during the day, and I dreamt about it at night. One day when I was standing at my locker, I wondered if I had California-on-the-brain syndrome when I thought I heard somebody say the words *San Diego.* I spun around to see if someone had really said it. There was this girl sitting against the wall talking to someone about where she had lived in San Diego. Without even thinking, I sat right down next to her.

"I'm going to San Diego!" I said. "You have to tell me all about it."

Of course the bell rang and I had to run before I got much more than her name, Rebecca, but as I ran to my next class it dawned on me: *Hey, she was really cute.* That day I didn't know that I had just met my future wife.

Rebecca was a junior. She had long, brown hair, big brown eyes that seemed to look straight into you, a beautiful smile, and the most wonderful laugh to go with it. At the beginning of that school year she had moved to Massachusetts from California. It's not unusual that we didn't meet earlier because there were about 3,000 students at North. So if I hadn't heard her say "San Diego" that day, it's likely we never would have met at all.

I tracked Rebecca down later that day. At that point I was less interested in her and more interested in finding out what she knew about San Diego. I found out that she had gone to the same high school as Tony Hawk. Even better, her best girlfriend in California was dating a pro skater named Laban Pheidias, whom I had seen in the magazines. This girl actually knew a pro skater! She was looking better and better to me.

A funny thing happened over the next week before I left for California. The more time that Rebecca and I spent talking, the less we talked about California. We started flirting with each other and leaving notes at each other's lockers. Before I knew it, I was starting to fall in love.

Spring Break in San Diego

I knew San Diego was for me the minute I walked off the plane. In the airport there were big pillars that held up the roof. At the bottom of the pillars were round cement areas that were perfect transitions. It was perfectly skateable, and it was the first thing I saw.

Although I didn't know anyone in California, I was lucky to know Chris Conway from Ratz skatepark in Maine. Conway ran a company called Who Skates. (The Who Skates team at the time included myself, Donny Barley, Matt Pailes, Jamal Williams, and Dan Drehoble—all pro skaters today.) When Conway heard I was going to San Diego, he called pro skater Chris Miller, who had come to Ratz for a demo once. He asked Miller to give me a place to stay for a night or two. I was so grateful to Chris Miller and his wife, Jen, for taking me in.

Miller picked me up at the airport in his Volkswagen van and gave me a tour of San Diego. It was a trip to see how different everything was. There were little bumps on the road between the lanes—you couldn't have those back in Boston because of

previous spread: The Flowrider is an awesome portable wave pool and probably the closest I'll ever come to surfing well.

the snowplows. There weren't very many trees, but the land-scape was beautiful to me and the constant, sunny, seventy-five-degree weather was calling me to stay. For the next two days I stayed at the Millers' house, went street skating with Chris, and fell in love with California.

The Millers were going away for the weekend, so when Friday rolled around, Chris said, "So where do you want me to take you to stay now?" It was a good question, but I didn't have an answer. I had just found out that the youth hostel where I thought I was going to stay was open only in the summer. The second one I knew about was pretty far in the south of San Diego, where there was no place to skate. But I knew I'd work something out, so I told him to drop me off at the Encinitas YMCA skatepark. I figured something would come to me while I skated the vert ramp.

There just happened to be a California Amateur Skateboard League (CASL) contest going on at the park that day. There were people all over the place. I was leaning on a fence watching the skaters with all my gear and bags at my feet when I saw some-body I knew! Across the park was Dave Metty, an old friend from Michigan.

"Hey, Dave!" I yelled as loudly as I could. "What are you doing here?"

It turns out that Dave had just moved to California and had landed a job filming promo videos of pro street skater Kris Markovich. He was living at the Blockhead house in Bonsal, about an hour northeast of downtown San Diego. Blockhead was a skateboard company that had the world-famous miniramp/bowl/spine combination behind a house that was known as a skaters' crash pad. All the skaters who came to the area and needed a place to stay went there. For the rest of my week in California I stayed at that house; I skated the miniramp and went street skating with some of the best skaters in California.

Although I was in there, I wasn't in style. As always, the East Coast was a bit behind the West Coast in fashion.

"You look lame," Markovich said with a laugh, looking me up and down as I stood there in my stonewashed Levi's jeans. "You can't come skating with us until we get you some clothes!"

Markovich gave me a double extra-large T-shirt and size forty "T-Bags" pants held up by a drawstring. "There," he said when I put them on. "Now we can go skating." I wore that outfit every day for the rest of the week.

This one-week trip was a turning point for me. I had dreamt about living in California and being a pro skater, but this was the first time I got an idea of what that life would be like. On the upside it was everything I thought it would be and more. The skaters were friendly and welcoming; the skate spots were the best in the country; and you couldn't beat the weather. But on the downside I started to suspect that pro skateboarding might be a lot more about who you know than how good you are. I went out there as a naive kid from New England who still thought that if I was good enough, I could be a pro. Now I had a nagging feeling there was more to it. But I put my worries aside and made the decision to definitely move to California after graduation.

Women Trouble

When I got back to Massachusetts, I couldn't wait to tell Rebecca about my trip. We began to spend every spare second together. She was different than any other girl I had dated. When I realized I was willing to give up some of my skating time for her, I knew I had fallen in love. Not that I stopped practicing every day, but if I said I would pick her up at seven, I would actually stop skating to be at her house on time.

At the end of the year I wrote Rebecca a love letter. I told her that I could picture spending the rest of my life with her. It was sappy and all, but that is how I felt, and it took a lot to put it all out there. Rebecca felt the same, but from her point of view, if I really loved her I wouldn't want to leave her and move to California. To me, it was just a little time apart until she finished school and came to live with me in California. I did love her, but I had to go.

My mom, too, didn't want me to go. She tried every argument, plea, and reason in the book. I wanted to make her happy and proud, but this time I just couldn't. After I graduated, I gave her a card that I made. On the front it said, *Mom, if you can open this card*

left: Hittin' some slalom gates on the hill next to my house.

in ten seconds without ripping it, I won't move to San Diego and I'll go to college and forget all this silly skateboard stuff. Then I taped, glued, stapled, sewed, tacked, padlocked, and secured the opening. On the back I wrote, *Sorry.* I was going.

The Infamous Letter

Just after I graduated high school and was getting ready to make my move to California, I wrote a letter to my family and friends. I'm not really sure why—maybe I was tired of answering the question of why I wasn't going to college. Whether or not they deserved an explanation, part of me wanted to give everyone one. I wrote the letter in the usual sarcastic, Teenage Mutant Ninja Turtles tone that was my trademark at the time. (Cowabunga!) It was full of the same dry humor that even today people have a hard time understanding. I wrote and mailed out copies of the letter without giving it too much thought. I even sent it to a few skaters in California that I didn't know very well. I just figured it was a good way to let them know I was going to be in town.

My family knew me and understood where I was coming from when I wrote things like, *Andy Macdonald, the skateboarder extraordinaire you all know and love.* But remarks like this were completely misunderstood by people in the skateboarding community. Taken literally, it sounded like I was some conceited jerk telling everyone, *Watch out! I'm coming to California to take over!* To them, the letter seemed so unbelievably weird that it was faxed out across the skate industry as a joke. Every team manager and bigwig in the business got to laugh at my little letter. I had become a laughingstock before I even left Boston. I didn't realize it at the time, but this guaranteed that any road to success as a professional skateboarder would be full of hardships and pitfalls. In my little New England world I still wanted to believe that if you were a good skateboarder, you would make it. I found out that this isn't at all the case.

That letter had such an impact on my career that it *still* pops up in the media every once in a while. It happened recently when I went to England to do a demo for SoBe Beverages. During a radio interview the deejay said, "Tell me about this letter." What!? I was blown away that this guy in England, who I had never met before, knew about a letter I had written to my family a decade earlier.

Although it caused me a lot of trouble (which I'll get to later), that letter has helped shape who I am and what I've become— not only in the world of skateboarding, but also in life.

part three:
california
dreamin'

9.

heading west

One day away from California, it dawned on me that I might just be out of my mind.

This is how I always imagined it would be: The principal would hand me my high school diploma. I would throw my graduation cap into the air, jump in my car, and tear out for California. But that's not how it happened. I needed more money to make the trip, so after graduation I got a job and didn't leave for California until October.

Getting Ready to Go

Right after graduation I moved up to Portland, Maine, to live on the couch of my friend, Chris Conway (who lived only twenty minutes from Ratz skatepark). Chris got me a job washing dishes at a country club for minimum wage. Although I was grateful for the work, it was a terrible job! A dish dog is the lowest of the low. The waitresses would dump a tray of dirty dishes in the sink. I'd have to separate the silverware from the dishes from the glasses, then hose them all off and put them in the dishwasher. Then, every fifteen minutes, the cooks would dump their sauté pans in the sink; those had to be washed by hand and returned immediately so the cooks could use them again. If I wasn't fast enough, the waitresses would run out of silverware and the cooks would run out of pans. Everybody ended up yelling at me. I'd go home around midnight, soaking wet, exhausted, and smelling like food and dirty dishwater. Then I'd sit down and write a letter to Rebecca.

This kind of life for a high school graduate who had no intentions of going on to college may not have looked too ambitious or successful to other people (namely, my mother), but I had a plan, and I knew I would be successful—eventually.

Woodward Camp

I was saved from the dishrag when I got a call from Woodward Camp in Pennsylvania. Woodward is a skateboarding and gymnastic camp for kids aged seven to seventeen, where I had worked the previous summer for three weeks. I had applied again this year hoping to be hired for the whole summer, but in the spring I was told I wasn't needed. Now they were in a pinch and offering me a job. Giving only two days' notice at the country club, I took off for Pennsylvania. I felt bad about leaving so quickly, but I figured I'd never need the club for a reference because I never wanted to wash dishes again.

At Woodward I was a counselor who taught kids how to skateboard. I slept in a cabin with twenty thirteen-year-olds; we woke up at 7:30, ate breakfast, and went off to skate. We'd work on the street course, then we'd head to the miniramp, then the bowl, and finally the vert ramp. I loved that job.

Woodward was also a stop for pros on their tours. They'd pull up in their vans when they were on the road and spend a couple days skating. There were also resident pros who spent the summer there and would do demos for the kids. This was a real bonus for me because, without actually competing against them, I was skating with most of the pros in the country before I was even a pro myself.

NSA '92

I took some time off from camp to compete in the National Skateboard Association competitions. That year I entered the northeast district contest and qualified in street, vert, and mini-ramp. I went to the regionals in Winston-Salem, North Carolina, and again qualified in miniramp and vert.

The national finals were in Houston, Texas, and for the second time many of my family members flew in to cheer me on. I needed it. Some of the best, who are still top skaters today, were there, including street skaters Andrew Reynolds and Matt Beach and vert skaters Matt Dove and Paul Zitzer.

One of the most memorable moments of the weekend was when Mirko Mangum (a pro skater for Planet Earth) saw that I had holes in my shoes. "Hey, dude," he said, "you can't skate in those. Here, put these on."

Mirko threw me an old pair of his Airwalks. I was so psyched. These were the greatest shoes—they didn't have holes in them and they were already broken in. And they must have been lucky: I got second place in miniramp and second in vert! It was a big improvement for me, and now people in the industry knew my name and they knew I could skate. Little did I know, though, they also connected my name to a certain letter they had heard about. On top of that they didn't like my helmet. I was still rocking an old-school Flyaway helmet, and back then skateboarders were pretty harsh fashion critics. But I ignored it. I wasn't going to change my style just because people heckled me.

Saying Good-bye

When camp ended at the beginning of September, I drove back to Boston. I wanted to say good-bye to everyone and pack up for my cross-country trip. Packing was easy—I didn't have that much stuff. I loaded two duffel bags full of clothes and I took three boards and my gear. That was it. I planned to sleep in the car, so I wanted to leave plenty of room for stretching out.

Then I said good-bye to my two favorite ladies—who were still both very unhappy about my plans to move to the other side of the country. My mother had finally accepted the fact that I

left: The indy nose bone is one of my favorite tricks.

was not going to college like my brother had—at least not right away. She figured that I'd go to California, learn the hard way that I couldn't make a living at skateboarding, and then come home and go to school. It's not that my mom didn't want to encourage my dreams. It's just that she was trying to be realistic. She wanted to guide me to a career where it would be easier to be self-supporting and happy. I love my mom for her good intentions and her doubts—they made me more driven to get out there and prove her wrong.

Then there was Rebecca. I made her brownies; I brought her flowers; I wrote her a poem. I swore I loved her and that we would be together when she graduated high school. But she still didn't want me to leave. It's hard to make a life-changing move when people you love and trust are telling you not to. But my desire to be a pro skater was so strong that I just had to go against their advice and head out by myself to my new home . . . 3,000 miles away.

Cross-Country

By the first week of October I was ready to go. My brother had given me a road atlas and my mom paid to fix her old Datsun wagon, which she'd given me as a graduation present. It was ancient and we all had our doubts that the car could make it across the country, but it was all I had, so off I went.

First Breakdown

When I pulled away from my mother's house, I was maybe a little sad and worried, but mostly, I was feeling great. I was off to California, and nothing was going to stop me now! This was awesome! This was the best! . . . Until my muffler was dragging on the ground just three hours into my cross-country drive. I exited the highway and pulled into the first gas station I found, which was closed and deserted. No problem—I broke out the duct tape, crawled under the car and taped the manifold to the exhaust.

What I didn't think about was that the heat of the pipe would melt the glue on the tape. One hour later the muffler was again dragging on the ground. But that was okay because I could drag it the short distance to my first scheduled stop in Connecticut, at my mother's sister's house. I had planned to stay there only one day—to say hello and then good-bye—but I ended up sitting around for two days waiting to get the car repaired. The delay was annoying, but what really bothered me was the expense. I had $1,000 in my pocket for this whole trip and to get an apartment in California. Now I was already down $200 and I'd only been gone a day! This wasn't the best way to start out.

Convoy

During my stay at Woodward, I had become good friends with a skater/counselor named Ozzie. He was now staying in Wellsville, Pennsylvania, with Buster Halterman (a pro skater from the late '80s). Ozzie had invited me to stop by to rest and skate Buster's barn ramp on my way out west. I left my aunt's house and headed out to the farm.

During my week in Wellsville, I met Shane, who was also at the farm on a stopover. He was a competitive snowboarder from South Carolina on his way to Colorado Springs to seek his own fortune. One afternoon when we finished skating and were resting on the front porch, I had an idea.

"Hey, Shane, want to travel with me?" I asked. "You could follow me up to my father's in Michigan. And then I could go with you down to Colorado."

"Sure," said Shane, without thinking twice. "That way, if our cars break down, we'll be there to save each other." I guess when you're traveling alone cross-country, it's easy to go with the flow.

My dad's home in Michigan was about a twelve-hour drive from there. Shane followed me out to Lansing, and we stayed for a night. My dad was happy about my trip. He probably believed, just like my mother, that I could never make a good living as a skateboarder, but he was glad that at least I had a plan. We hugged each other, smiled at the camera, and then said good-bye. Shane and I were off to Colorado.

A Long Stretch of Road

Shane and I checked the map to see how far Colorado was from Michigan. The distance was what we called a "double shakka." If you put your thumb on Michigan, curled in your middle three fingers, and then extended out your pinkie finger, you'd be

halfway there. We had to cross through Illinois, Indiana, the long stretch of Nebraska, and Iowa. It was a full two days' drive. Today that's not such a big deal for me, but at that time both Shane and I had cars that threatened to self-destruct if they went over fifty-five miles an hour. That kept us in the slow lane on the right as we drove twelve hours each day.

When you drive for hours on end, it's easy to start seeing things that make you think you're going crazy. One night in Nebraska, I was out in front on a single-lane highway with my high beams on. I was driving along at what for us was top speed when I thought I saw something in the road ahead. I wasn't too concerned; I figured it was probably just my imagination. But as I got closer the object got bigger. Suddenly, I saw, right in the middle of the road, an armchair. It must have fallen off a truck and was sitting there, perfectly upright and facing me directly. If someone had been sitting in it, we'd be face-to-face. I swerved out into the oncoming traffic lane with my lights flashing and horn blowing, hoping Shane would follow me and miss the chair too. He did, and fortunately, there was no oncoming traffic. That's the interesting thing about a trip like this. You just don't know what to expect, so you can't prepare for everything. No one offering advice would have said, *Watch out for armchairs on the highway.*

They might have warned me about the loneliness and fatigue factor, however. It takes a lot of mental endurance to make this kind of cross-country trip. There are stretches of road in the Midwest that just go on forever. The road disappears far in front of you at the horizon, and it's very hard to stay focused. I would start staring at the white line in the road and then feel myself drifting off to sleep.

The long stretches of road also gave me time to relax a bit— maybe too much. When Shane and I got to the middle of Iowa, I pulled a joke to break up the monotony. We were on a double-lane highway, and I was behind him. I put my left foot on the gas pedal and my left hand on the steering wheel. Then I slid over to the passenger's seat and rested my head against the window, pretending to be asleep. I pulled the car up next to Shane, and

previous spread: Just like Evel Knievel.

when he looked over, he went nuts. He started beeping his horn and yelling, "Andy! Wake up! What are you doing?" I jumped alert, as if just awakened, and then laughed my head off for the next ten minutes.

Finally, we pulled into the trailer park in Colorado Springs where Shane's friends lived. It had occurred to me (having had lots of time to think while driving) that I really had no idea what I would do when I finally reached California. So I stayed with Shane and his friends for a day. We cruised around town on scooters wearing our skate helmets and we sessioned the ramp behind Shane's friends' trailer. I was having a good time, and I wasn't in a hurry to get back on the road.

I Made It!

Even though Shane had been in his own car, at least he was with me. Now, as I pulled out of the trailer park, I felt alone for the first time. I was headed into the Rocky Mountains, and that's a tough drive. At the steep mountain passes there are signs that say: TURN OFF YOUR AIR CONDITIONER. If you don't, you're bound to overheat. I didn't have to pay any attention to those signs because I didn't have an air conditioner. But I did have to worry about overheating every time I headed uphill. My radiator was broken, so my engine had no way of cooling itself. My car just couldn't exert that much power without breaking down.

I crept along slowly in the right lane (with all the trucks) with my flashers on. Then I turned my heater on full blast. This drew the heat away from the engine and reduced the risk of overheating. It made for one miserable ride sitting on plastic seats. But even with all these precautions, every once in a while the Datsun would still overheat. I'd pull off the road for about a half hour, let the car cool down, fill it back up with water, and then take off again. Good thing I'm a patient person.

Finally, I made it to the other side of the Rockies and out into the desert of Nevada (where I still had to keep my heater running in ninety-degree weather to keep the car going!). I spent my first night by myself and my last night on the road at a desert rest stop. That night I was scared. The very next day I would be in San Diego. I would begin my new life. And I hadn't a plan, a clue, or an idea about how I was going to do it. Back in Boston that hadn't seemed like a problem. But now, one day away from California, it dawned on me that I might just be out of my mind. Even still, I couldn't wait for the morning.

At daybreak I pulled onto Interstate 5 South and drove straight ahead to my future. Then there it was—a sign far ahead in the distance: WELCOME TO SAN DIEGO COUNTY. The way I reacted, you would have thought it said: YOU'VE JUST WON A MILLION BUCKS! I had driven 3,000 miles in a broken car just to read that sign. I didn't know anyone. I didn't know where I was going or what I was going to do next, but with high hopes and about five hundred bucks left in my pocket, I was the happiest kid in the world.

10.
carving out a living
When you're at the bottom, at least you know which way is up.

I couldn't believe it—I was in California! To me, that was the first step to becoming a pro skater. I was going to prove to all who ever doubted me (and, most importantly, to myself) that I could do this. I exited I-5 at Encinitas Boulevard and drove straight to the YMCA skatepark to admire the vert ramp. It wasn't open yet, so I went down to Street Life skate shop—it was the only other place in San Diego I knew how to get to and somewhere I thought I might find some skaters.

What I remember most about this visit to Street Life was that everyone was really mean. I went in naive and high on life, and I came out thinking that maybe this wasn't such a good idea. It was 1992, and skateboarding was in the middle of some of its darkest days. Pro skaters earned only a couple hundred dollars a month, and vert skating was out. Street skating was king, and tricks had become so technical that in order to do them you needed smaller wheel sizes so that the board would flip faster, which meant that everyone skated very slowly. From the tricks you did to the size and style of the clothes you wore, skaters were now focused more on what was cool than on what was challenging—and, more importantly, on what was fun.

"Hey, what's up? Do you know what time the park opens?" I asked the guy behind the counter.

He took one look at my board, with its large wheels, and laughed. "Nobody skates vert anymore," he said. "Why would you want to go to that lame park, anyway?"

I decided not to mention that I'd just driven 3,000 miles in hopes of becoming a pro and to skate the vert ramp at that "lame park."

Jobless and No Place to Stay

When the park opened at 3:00 P.M., I gladly paid my two dollars and skated for the whole session. It felt good to skate and get my mind off that nagging question in the back of my head: *Now what?*

After the session I called Rebecca's best friend, Aimee Shattuck. She lived in Solana Beach, about ten minutes south of the park, and Rebecca had told her I was coming. Aimee, her mother, and her younger brother, Damon, shared a small two-bedroom apartment just off the highway. The Shattucks welcomed me with open arms, fed me dinner, and asked me lots of questions about Rebecca and her new home in Boston. They said I could stay with them for a while, and I was very grateful— but also uncomfortable. Damon was already sleeping on the couch in the living room, so although they were being very kind to let me stay, there really was no room. I felt like an intruder, but I had no other options. I accepted their kind offer, explaining that I planned to get a job right away and move on.

The next morning I went out early to find a place of my own. After looking at the apartment listings in the newspaper, I realized that it was going to take a little more than the $500 I had to get started. I applied for at least six jobs that first day. I went to a gas station, a grocery store, fast-food places, and a Blockbuster video store. I thought the job at the video store

right: This pool is behind a Baptist church. I hooked the minister up with a bunch of SoBe swag and he let me ride for hours.

© Brittain

would be a cinch. I already had a year's experience in the business back in Newton. I went back for two interviews, but in the end, I got beat out by someone else. I had no idea jobs at Blockbuster were so competitive!

A week went by and still no job. Money was going quick, even though I ate only one meal a day: a ninety-nine-cent red burrito and a small fountain drink with free refills from Del Taco. And already I felt like I had overstayed my welcome at the Shattucks'.

On the Floor with Bacon

It was a long shot, but I kind of knew a guy named Bacon who lived in the area. I had first met "Bacon" (John Hobbs) at Maximus back in Massachusetts. We weren't friends or anything, but about a year earlier he was at the park and I was telling him about my plans to move to California. I found out he was moving there too. Before he left that day, he'd said, "Here's the number where I'll be in California; call me when you get there."

I saw Bacon again when I went to California on spring break. It was during a heated session on the vert ramp at the Encinitas skatepark. It was my first time skating with pros in California, and I wanted to skate my absolute best to try to stand out a little. I was really into my skating when Bacon came over to say hello. I was psyched to see that he'd made it to San Diego and seemed to be doing well. I figured that if he could do it, I could do it too. He introduced me to his roommate, Chris Rooney ("Rhino"). Rhino was not the kind of guy who would blend into a crowd. He was six foot three, had lots of tattoos, and hair down to the middle of his back. Bacon told me that Rhino was from Boston too. I said hello, but as Rhino tells it, I totally blew him off. Here were these two guys from Boston trying to make friends with a kid from their home turf, and all I was thinking about was my next run.

Now I was back in San Diego, and so I gave Bacon a call. He took me to a backyard pool in Del Mar—the first of countless pools I'd skate in Southern California. At the end of the day I asked him if I could sleep on his floor until I found a job. Bacon didn't think twice. "No worries!" he said right away. I grabbed my gear from Aimee's, said my good-byes with loads of thanks, and went down to Bacon's.

Bacon lived in Ocean Beach (the first beach north of downtown San Diego). He had a two-bedroom apartment that he shared with Rhino. Rhino wasn't too thrilled about me being there. I was the guy from Boston who had brushed him off the first time we met. I could see when he said hello that he was really thinking, *Oh, great. I have to live with this kook?* (It's funny that after such a bad start Rhino and I became the best of friends and housemates for eight years.)

We were all pretty short on cash. Rhino and I were both unemployed, and Bacon worked at a Subway shop. He wasn't making a lot of money, but he did get some free sandwiches and extra lunch meat to bring home once in a while, so that helped.

A few weeks later I still didn't have a job, but it wasn't from lack of trying. I went out every day applying for any job I could find. As a former dish dog, I had no shame. I would mop the floor, clean the bathroom, shovel poop, anything! I had only enough money to fill up my car with gas a few more times. I was hungry and really tired of eating sandwich fixings.

Rhino and I solved our food problem when we found a bar in Mission Beach called the Red Onion. Every evening they would have a happy hour with free finger food. The idea was that you'd buy drinks while you ate rolled tacos and socialized. Rhino and I had a different idea—we were going in for the free food.

The first step in our mission was to sneak me in the back door. (I was only nineteen and not allowed in a bar.) Once we were in, all we had to do was keep moving. We'd sit down in other people's chairs in front of their drinks while they were up at the buffet so the waitress would think we were paying customers. When we saw the waitress coming around to take another drink order, we'd move over to the buffet table to stuff our faces. It was just a matter of moving to the right place at the right time and looking like we belonged there.

Before I knew it, I had been in California for three weeks and it was Halloween. Rhino invited me to come with him to a Halloween party at the Powell skatepark up in Santa Barbara. I don't know if Rhino really wanted me to tag along, but my car was more likely than his to make the trip, so I drove. We got there, and I thought it had to be the greatest place on earth. There were skeletons and ghouls riding around on skateboards.

© Tommy Cook

above: Ice-T came to a party we had at the Human warehouse.

There was a mummy with his body wrappings trailing behind him as he skated by. I was unemployed, sleeping on the floor every night, and stealing food, but moments like this made it all worthwhile. The way I figured it, when you're at the bottom, at least you know which way is up.

Paychecks

Rhino and I both knew we had to start making some money. We signed on with a temporary employment agency while we were looking for more long-term work. On our first job Rhino and I got paid to stand on a street corner in downtown San Diego from 5:30 A.M. to 9:00 A.M. passing out free samples of a new product by Quaker Oats called Oat Cups. The job paid about eight bucks an hour (more than I'd ever made!), plus we got to fill our kitchen cabinet with microwavable Oat Cups. We did this for a couple weeks, and although it doesn't sound too exciting, Rhino and I were psyched to be working and to still have the whole day to skate.

After the Oat Cups gig I demoed the Miracle Piano at Price Clubs in and around San Diego. I had to wear a shirt and tie for this one, so I went down to a thrift store and spent three bucks on an outfit. I had never played the piano in my life, but that was the miracle—no experience or talent was necessary. It was a self-teaching keyboard that came with software that you could hook up to your computer. I even learned a few songs before the gig was up.

These jobs were good, but not so good. They weren't consistent enough to pay for an apartment. So I kept my spot on the floor at Rhino and Bacon's place and kept looking for a steady job. Near Ocean Beach there's an area called Hotel Circle. It's a two-mile loop of hotels, restaurants, and a convention center. I figured I had to be able to find a job in there. (Now I regretted that I didn't have a recommendation from my dishwashing job in Maine.) I could be a bellhop, a waiter, a receptionist. I could do housekeeping, maintenance, yard work, or whatever would bring in a paycheck. I went to over twenty hotels and filled out applications but couldn't get a job; nobody was hiring.

I was driving home that evening feeling unusually run down and defeated. I had been in California for almost a month, and I

© RHINO

still had not found a real job, let alone the hard stuff like an apartment or a skateboard sponsorship. Now I was questioning myself. Could I really do this? Everyone back home had told me I couldn't. Is it possible they had been right? As I was going over all this in my mind, I passed the entrance to Sea World. Sea World! Why hadn't I thought of that? I pulled into the parking lot thinking they must have a job opening on a sweep-up crew.

The board on the front of the employment office listed two jobs. *Wow!* I thought. *They're hiring.* One was for a marine biologist with a college degree (that wouldn't do), and the other was for a walk-around character. Dressing up like some kind of cartoon character and getting paid for it? That sounded more like me! So I went in and filled out an application. I knew I'd be good with kids because I was one.

The secretary read my application and looked me over. She seemed so impressed that I actually wanted this job that she made a phone call and got me an immediate interview. (I guess not everyone thinks that walking around in the heat all day in a forty-five-pound furry costume with kids jumping all over you is the best job opportunity!)

They handed me a whale costume and asked me to try it on. I loved it! I started dancing around, and the interviewer grabbed my flipper. "Whoa," he said. "Calm down. Okay, okay, you're hired." They set me up with a stylin' polyester uniform, complete with a Sea World jacket. I never asked how much the job paid; I just wanted it. I went home and proudly told Rhino and Bacon that I was Shamu!

When I arrived for work the first day, I found out that Shamu didn't walk among the crowds much because it was too dangerous. The last Shamu blew out his knee when he was tackled by a little kid. So they gave me a bodyguard who could warn me when a kid was coming at me too fast. "Incoming at three o'clock!" he'd say. The suit had flipper feet and was eight feet high and very top-heavy. If I started to lean over, I was going down. I spent most of my time in the photo booth, where kids would sit on my lap and have their picture taken. I was sort of like the Santa of Sea World.

left: Flipping out at home in my backyard.

The job cut into my skate time a bit, but I worked only four days a week, and that left three for skating. Not only did I have a paycheck, but I got a bonus: That Thanksgiving everyone who worked at Sea World got a free turkey. How stoked was I?! $4.75 an hour and a free turkey. I was coming up!

skate for fun

We all skateboard for a million different reasons, but first and foremost, we do it because it's fun—because we love to do it. To me, that's the most important thing about skateboarding. From kids helping each other learn tricks on the street to pros cheering on their fellow competitors, skateboarders have done a great job holding fast to this lesson and handing it down. It is one of the things that makes me proud to be a skater. I see too many mainstream sports today destroying themselves mostly because the athletes have forgotten why they started playing to begin with: for the joy of it.

Sick and Twisted

I stayed at Sea World until the following March, when a better job came along with a company called Spike and Mike's Festival of Animation. Rhino and I were hired to hand out advertising flyers for their films as they traveled around. Their show, named *Sick and Twisted,* was attracting lots of attention. This is where *Beavis and Butthead, Ren & Stimpy*, and *South Park* all began. Their festival was coming to San Diego and San Francisco, and we were hired to promote it.

Handing out flyers for Spike and Mike's was different from just standing on corners handing out samples of Oat Cups. Rhino and I went around to record stores, college campuses, amusement parks, or anywhere there might be people interested in animated films. We'd also grab attention by putting on street shows that would make people stop for a minute so they would take our flyers. Once, on the campus at U.C. Berkeley, we stopped traffic to put on a cow race. We had bought dozens of little battery-operated cows that could walk, moo, and wag their tails.

"Cow races! Cow races!" we'd yell. "Place your bets right here!"

This would draw a huge crowd, and after the race most people were glad to take our flyers and hear about the *Sick and Twisted* show. We found out we were very good at making a spectacle out of nothing.

This was a good job, but I still wasn't happy. Almost a year had passed, and I hadn't moved any closer to my goal of skating for a living. That had to change.

part four:
california
pro

11.
paid to skate

I made a copy of my contract and wrote, "I TOLD YOU SO!" on the front in big red letters and sent it to my mom.

In the early 1990s, pro skateboarders were not making big bucks, but at least they were making enough to pay the rent—which was more than I could say for myself. To be a pro I had to get a skateboard company not only to give me gear, but also to give me my own signature board. But this was taking more time and was a lot harder than I had planned. In fact, there were so many things working against me that sometimes I wondered if it just wasn't meant to be.

The Final NSA Finals

I pinned my hopes on winning the '93 NSA finals so I could finally go pro. Unlike other sports, there are no criteria for being a pro skateboarder. Generally, a pro is someone who is paid by a sponsor and has a signature board with that company. In the past skaters who did well at the NSA finals always picked up a sponsor, if they didn't already have one, and turned pro thereafter. But that wasn't happening for me. In '92, I had won second place in vert and second in miniramp, but I still had no sponsors. Maybe this year it would be different.

That summer I left California to work again at Woodward Camp in Pennsylvania. I took time off for the NSA regional contest and qualified again for the finals in vert and miniramp. This time the finals were held back at the Encinitas YMCA. So along with Donny Barley, a friend who was also competing, I flew back to California. (My car had made its last cross-country trip; it wasn't going back to the West Coast ever again.)

I won first place in vert and second in miniramp. In years past that would have gotten me a sponsor on the spot, but not anymore. Skateboarding was still in a slump. Even the NSA went out of business after that competition, and because vert skating especially was dead, not many companies wanted to crank out boards that weren't going to sell. So they didn't need someone like me to help promote them.

Selling Myself

If sponsors weren't coming to me, I figured I'd go to them. I put together a portfolio of my skateboarding experience. I included a list of all the contests I'd entered, and I added magazine photos and stories that included my name. Then I walked around the Action Sports Retailer trade show and gave out copies to all the companies I thought I'd like to ride for. At this point I would have been happy to find a company that would give me free boards— never mind a signature board. I had been skating a cracked deck for three months, and it was driving me crazy. With the amount of skating I was doing, I could have used a new deck at least every month, not to mention trucks, wheels, and bearings.

Soon I realized that there was something else working against me. Remember that letter I wrote when I left high school? The one that got faxed out all over the industry? Well, here it was back to haunt me. My infamous letter had given me a reputation that made company owners wary of sponsoring me. They thought I had an "attitude," so they wouldn't touch me. Once again I faced the prejudice of being an outsider, which had been pretty severe in my conservative New England town.

Even now out in California, where I had thought I would easily fit in, people were making judgments about me before they'd even met me.

Finally, one company agreed to flow me clothes and boards. It was Chapter 7, run by Mike McGill, who was one of the original members of the Bones Brigade. Mike wasn't going to make me a pro, but he hooked me up with all the product I needed to keep skating.

Eureka?

When I returned to California for the NSA finals I was excited about the competition, but I was more excited about Rebecca being out there too. She had graduated high school and returned to the West Coast. I couldn't wait to see her and start over again. We had kept in close touch over the past year. I didn't have the money to call her often, and there was no such thing as e-mail back then, but I had written her a letter (and sometimes two) every day.

As soon as I got off the plane, I took a bus to Aimee's house, where Rebecca was staying. We were so happy to see each other—lots of hugs and smiles. Then in a by-the-way conversation she told me that she was moving to Eureka. Eureka!? That's a fifteen-hour drive north of San Diego. It was like someone just scratched the needle across a record and stopped the music. How come I didn't know anything about this? I thought she came out here to be with me? I guess because my letters read more like a journal of what I had been doing rather than a love story, Rebecca had assumed we were just friends. I was so into my skating that she thought I was over having her as a girlfriend. Well, I wasn't. I left the room quickly to compose myself. Then I went back and said something like, "Well, I've got to get to the contest now. See ya." And that was the last time I saw Rebecca before she moved north. I guess I did a good job of hiding my feelings because she didn't know until years later that she had broken my heart that day.

My Own Apartment

In the fall of '93 things started to look up—a little. With the money I had earned at Woodward and my job with Spike and

Rocket air á la Christian Hosoi
at a nighttime session in
Mission Valley.

© RHINO

top: Slob fastplant at Maximus in Cambridge, Massachusetts, with my brother looking on.

left: Hurricane grind at Brent's ramp.

above: Me, Jody, and Christian in Boston, Massachusetts, after finishing the 20-mile "Walk for Hunger."

right: Stalefish over the hip at Hastings Park in Vancouver, British Columbia.

bottom right: Life on the road: e-mail, digi camera, cell phone, CDs, pizza and cranberry juice for dinner, and a pint of Ben and Jerry's for dessert.

bottom left: In the second grade I thought I was a cat. Check out those fangs.

below: Rebecca and me at the 2002 Transworld Awards.

© RHINO

Flatground kickflip at home in Ocean Beach

right: My fire pole is the fastest way down to the presents on Christmas morning. I even got Mom to go down (feet first).

bottom right: In the closing ceremonies of the 1996 Olympics in Atlanta, Georgia, we did a demo in front of 85,000 people with two-thirds of the globe watching on TV. I was a little nervous. Left to right: Brian Howard, Adil Dyani, Tony Hawk, Mike Frazier, Mike Crum, Steve Caballero, Tom Boyle, me, Daren Mendido, Neal Hendrix.

bottom left: Visiting Mom while on tour in Boston in '97.

above left: Packing up the Datsun in San Diego, California, to head back east to skate camp.

above right: When I was on *The Tonight Show* I came out skating and ollied onto Jay Leno's desk. Rebecca, Jay, and me.

right: Frontside 180 over a gap in San Diego, California.

© Brittain

© Brittain

above: Sometimes I miss.

right: In the spring of '97, I was the first to do a backflip over a jump box. At the X Games that year, I did it at the end of my street run.

Mike's, I was able to get my own apartment. I found a three-bedroom unit in the ghetto of Ocean Beach. I put down the security deposit, signed a six-month lease and then brought in Donny and his two friends from Connecticut to split the rent. I also put my life savings into a "new," sun-faded maroon 1985 Honda Civic. The car was a lemon from the start. It had fake tinted windows and furry purple seat covers, but it got me and my friends where we needed to go. I also got a job working at a surf shop (though I didn't surf) called The Green Room in Ocean Beach. It didn't pay as much as Spike and Mike's, but at least I was home more and could spend more time skating.

Having my own place was a step up for me, but not a giant step. There wasn't one piece of furniture in the whole apartment. So not only was I still sleeping on the floor, I was now also sitting and eating on the floor. Our place quickly became a hangout for lots of people I didn't know, and it turned into a really nasty place. People would drop the sticky, tarlike backing from their grip tape onto the rug when setting up new boards and just leave it there. Fast-food leftovers were all over the place and made a real feast for the roaches that lived with us. I soon started to hate it.

This was the lowest time for me. I had some serious doubts about my dreams ever coming true. I remember sitting in my room alone on Christmas Day, thinking about how everything had turned out. I was hungry all the time; I had no money and no prospects for making it big. My mother always told me that I could come home anytime, but the stubborn side of me just wouldn't let me do that. I had to prove to her and especially to myself, that I could make it on my own.

Going Pro

In the winter of 1994, I went to skate a vert ramp that was in the warehouse of a company called Thruster that made wakeboards and snowboards. After skating a few nights, I met the owner, Tom Carter. I didn't know it at the time, but this meeting would change my life.

Tom wanted to start a skateboard division and wondered if I wanted to help him do it. I didn't want to be a businessman; I wanted to be a skateboarder. But I did know someone who might be interested. Ozzy Alvarez was a pro for a small board company called Entity. He already had a lot of connections in the industry, but he wasn't happy. He agreed to leave that job and help me create a new company under Thruster. I finally had a sponsor willing to turn me pro!

Soon Ozzy and I were putting together a team of riders and drawing up a business plan for Tom. We all agreed to name the company "Human." I drew up the logo, which was the word *HUMAN* printed in block letters, with the *A* looking like a paper doll cutout with a head, arms, and legs. During this time I was walking around in a daze just thinking about actually being a pro—a real pro, one of the guys I had always admired, one of the guys who could make a living as a skateboarder, one of the guys everybody told me I would never be. Human skateboards debuted in the spring of 1994 with Ozzy Alvarez and Andy Macdonald as pros.

I signed a contract with Human/Thruster for $1,200 per month. That doesn't seem like much today, but at the time that first check was almost more money than I'd made in the whole previous year. I was stoked! To earn this money, all I had to do was ride the Human board and go to contests and demos. This was it! I made a copy of my contract and wrote *I TOLD YOU SO!* on the front in big red letters and sent it to my mom.

Right away I quit my other jobs. I was a pro skater now, and my job was to skate. I also moved out of the roach palace . . . at a price. Because my name was on the lease that we were breaking, I had to pay a penalty fee, put in a new rug, paint the walls, cover the overdue phone bill, and forfeit my security deposit. But it was worth it to get into my new place. Rhino and I found a two-bedroom apartment closer to the beach that had termites but no roaches—much better.

In May, I went to my first pro contest at the Slam City Jam in Vancouver, British Columbia. Human paid for my airfare and hotel. This was the way to go! I placed fifth and proved to myself that I really could compete with pros and make some money. I earned about $300 that day and used it to get to my next contest. That became my method for many future competitions. I

right: Slob air in the bowl at my home park in Clairemont.

would skate well enough to make the top ten cut to the finals—the money round. Then I would skate just well enough in the finals to place somewhere in the middle, like fifth or sixth. To aim for first or second, I'd have to be more aggressive and risk a fall that could put me out of placing completely; I couldn't afford to do that. So I stayed in the middle and earned enough money to get a plane ticket to the next contest and still have some left over to pay my bills.

If Thruster had been as organized and professional as I first thought it was, I wouldn't have had to invent this financial system—the company would have been paying my way to these contests. But that wasn't the case. My first clue that Thruster might not be as great as I thought came when I was on my way to Europe for my first overseas contests. I was supposed to ride street and vert on a Friday in England. Thruster booked the plane ticket and got me as far as St. Louis, Missouri. At the stopover I was supposed to pick up my prepaid ticket for England, but it wasn't paid for! I called Tom in a panic and got him to wire money right away, but I missed my flight and missed my first European street contest. Eventually, I got there, and I went from England to Germany for the world championships (and placed third in vert and seventh in street). I then went to France and skated the Marseille bowls for the first time. To this day that is one of my favorite places in the world to skate.

Things like the unpaid plane ticket happened all the time with Thruster. Sometimes I'd go months without a paycheck at all. But fortunately, I picked up some other sponsors who helped keep me going. I had been on the flow team for Airwalk (meaning they gave me shoes but no money), but now I was on the A team and getting paid. Gullwing Trucks and Bald Clothing also helped me out and paid for some great trips. In '94, Bald flew me and a couple other guys to Japan for a week-long clothing trade show. It was my first time ever to Asia. We did a demo at the show in Tokyo and then went to Komakora to go surfing. Except for the moment when I thought I was going to drown in the waters stirred up by a coming monsoon, I was having a blast.

Back at home my roommates and I would skate the YMCA Missile Park ramp during the day, come home and eat huge plates of pasta, and then go down to the Human ramp for the night session. Because of skateboarding, I was traveling all over the world, skating the best places on earth, and making money doing it. It was all I ever wanted, but I knew it could be better.

First Pro Win

At the start of the '95 season I won my first pro contest. I went up to Sacramento for a Pro Skateboard League contest at The Grind skatepark. It was a street event and the course was in the parking lot. I was staying with my teammate, Ozzy, and he and his friend Jeff Tolland kept me up until five in the morning the night before the contest, fooling around and creating havoc in the hotel room. I remember thinking, as I finally fell asleep, that there was no way I was going to be able to skate very well the next day.

As it turned out, I skated well enough to earn my first-ever pro victory. I beat out Eric Koston, who finished second. I guess some people weren't too happy to lose to this new kid who was better known as a vert skater. Right away people started chiding me about everything from the tricks I chose to do to the color of my helmet and T-shirt to the way I wore my shoes. But then and now, I couldn't have cared less.

Skateboarding's Comeback

By midseason in 1995, skateboarding began to make a comeback in popularity. This was especially obvious at the first ESPN X Games in Providence, Rhode Island. The event was broadcast on ESPN, and it brought a lot of much-needed attention to the sport—but you should have seen the way they put together a skatepark. They had a pink street course with little swirly designs painted all over it. The ramps were terrible because they were built to look good on TV, but they were not at all good for skating on. But still, it was a really exciting event that helped put skateboarding back on the map.

Tony Hawk won the vert that year, and I got my typical sixth place. It was obvious that skating was on an upswing again, but at that moment I had no idea just how good it was going to get for me the following year.

12.
the turning point
When I'm really into it and skating well, my body just takes over.

It was my third summer on the pro tour, but I was still having trouble being accepted in the industry. My "squeaky-clean" image and my refusal to go with the flow of what was considered cool wasn't helping any. I was still the same spastic kid from Boston I'd always been. I wasn't one to hold back my excitement about things and play the cool guy—especially when it came to skating. I didn't care when or where or what we skated, I just wanted to skate. While other pros were at the who's-who industry parties, I was skating backyard pools with Rhino and our new East Coast roommates, Preston and Ozzie. (Pool skating hadn't been cool since the late '80s.) Just like when I first started, I didn't have any tattoos or even the right haircut. I didn't do drugs, smoke, or drink. I was just me, and that wasn't the kind of person most people expected a skateboarder to be.

Although I was always confident in who I was and what I believed in, all the negativity was wearing. I found myself wondering again if I was really cut out for this pro skateboarder stuff. I was there. I was doing just fine at fifth and sixth place in contests, but I wanted to be the best—and I was having doubts that I had it in me anymore. Then in 1996, I beat Tony Hawk in the X Games, and suddenly things started to turn around.

1996 ESPN X Games

It was only the second year of the X Games, but already the event had surpassed even ESPN's hopes of how successful it would become. The Games were held at the Newport Yachting Club in Rhode Island right on the water, and there were so many fans, they had to stop letting people in hours before the events even started. Up to that point Tony Hawk had dominated vert contests. I, on the other hand, was still a rookie and had managed only one pro victory so far—and it was in a street contest. I had no reason to think I'd come out on top, but I did feel like I had something to prove. Critics were saying that my vert skating wasn't very powerful and that I didn't go very high. I was going to change that.

The qualification round was much like any other contest, with the exception of the huge crowds and cameras in your face everywhere you turned. I skated my usual conservative run, doing only four-foot airs and skipping the more risky flip tricks. This was good enough to qualify me in sixth place out of the ten spots in the final.

goin' for a whirlybird

The waiting during a contest is always the worst part, but at the '96 X Games there was an interesting diversion. The Games were created by ESPN and made for television, but back then the announcers didn't know anything about skateboarding. ESPN had tried to get their sportscasters, who were used to mainstream sports, to quickly learn skateboarding lingo. The effort wasn't very successful, but it was funny. Skateboarding, along with its complex and sometimes senseless terminology, can't simply be learned in a crash course. One has to live it. The announcers would yell, "Oh, there's a nice boardslide," when the guy was doing a backside grind. The broadcast coverage was pretty dodgy too: "Is it a chill in the air or a chill down your spine? The skaters have taken the vert ramp for the finals!" Were they serious?! It was just too easy to mess with these guys. They'd ask us on camera, "What do you have planned for this run?" Pretending to be very serious, we'd make up stuff like, "If I make the whole run, I'm goin' for a whirlybird at the end," which is totally not a trick, but the announcers would be waiting for this grand whirlybird finale. The whole thing was supercheesy, but at least it helped pass the time.

First Pro Vert Win

The next day I went up to the ramp to practice for the finals and consciously reminded myself to take it easy. In the past I would practice so hard that by the time the finals started, my legs would be Jell-O. This time I just warmed up a bit and waited. After about another half hour the contest started. Every skater had three runs, with only the best one counting toward the final score. My first run was a good one, and I had the lead until Tony Hawk skated and beat my score. No one was surprised—every-one expected him to win. I took my second run and fell on a kick flip indy, so that was a throwaway run right there. By the time I got to my third run, I was tied for second place with Mike Frazier and Tony was still in first. At that point I knew my third run had to be my absolute best. I wasn't going for the win; I just wanted to hold on to second.

I started my run with high tweaked airs, a big 540, and some flip tricks. The judges, who were used to seeing me skate at a three- or four-foot level, were now seeing me at a five- or six-foot level. At the end I did a combination that included a varia-tion of another 540, straight into a board varial, then a 360 varial, and then I ended with a flip trick to fakie right on the buzzer. It was my best run.

People sometimes ask me what's going through my head when I'm skating under pressure like that. Most of the time the answer is "Nothing." When I click my tail out and they announce my name, I get supernervous. The feeling usually lasts for the first two or three walls. If I'm not skating well, the feeling lasts longer and I think about every single move. I analyze what just happened and what I have to do next. When that happens, I know my score is going to be pretty low. But when I'm really into it and skating well, my body just takes over and I don't think about the routine step-by-step. It all becomes one forty-five-second trick—one movement of my body. On that third run I was in the zone, and I scored an 89.0 out of a possible 100. I was now back in the lead.

The pressure was on, and Tony knew he had to step it up. He was at a slight disadvantage because, at the time, he didn't do any flip tricks in his contest runs and I had just done three. It's really hard to be consistent with flip tricks, and they're a lot more risky. If you watch what most skaters fall on, nine times out of ten it's the flip tricks. As you come off the top of the ramp, you're kicking the board away from you, and if you grab it wrong or can't grab it at all, you're done. So judges consider that in the scoring.

When Tony's scores came up after his final run, he had pulled an 88.33. I had edged him out by only a few tenths of a point, and everyone in the place (including me) was shocked. I had finally claimed my first pro vert win! Right away there was a frenzy of ESPN people running around like something terrible had just happened. They were yelling things like, "Are those scores right?" "Has Andy ever beat Tony?" "Has Andy ever won a pro vert contest before?" "Andy who?"

Someone stuck a microphone in my face and asked, "How does it feel to beat Tony Hawk?" I was still in shock and stuttered something about being surprised and feeling great. For Tony's part, he was incredibly gracious; he said it seemed that for a long time people hadn't appreciated my style of skating. He said he was glad to see that I was finally getting some recognition. That meant more to me than winning the contest.

After all the interviews and the autograph signing, my family and I were the last ones at the yacht club. I was flying. My family was there with me, and I had just won more money than I had ever won in a contest. I yelled, "I just won five grand and I'm taking everyone out to dinner!"

my first 540

Sometimes my most awesome sense of accomplishment comes the first time I land a trick I've been working on. I still remember where I was and exactly how I felt the first time I made a successful 540.

I was working at Woodward during the summer of 1994. It was the Fourth of July, and about 300 campers and staff had gathered to watch a big demo on the vert ramp. Toward the end of my session I decided to try a 540 just to see how it felt. After trying for six years, I felt I was really close to getting it that summer. The hardest part about learning 540s at first is simply trying them without being scared to death. By now I could spin them pretty much whenever I wanted without the fear factor, but I still couldn't land one.

On that first attempt I held the board to my feet longer than I usually did before bailing out. It felt really good. I had a solid grab, and I spotted my landing early. But I still couldn't get myself to set it down. After a few more tries the crowd around the ramp started to get behind me. Many of the other staffers had seen me out at the vert ramp trying 540s for hours. That day they screamed and cheered louder and louder, and with each try, I came closer and closer. By about the seventh or eighth attempt the crowd was on their feet before I even dropped in. The cheering intensified as I set up on the first wall with a backside air. By this point not only did I want to land this trick for myself, I wanted to land it for them, too.

I chucked off the lip a little harder and a little higher but, most of all, with a little more confidence. Before I knew what had happened, I was skating across the flat bottom and everyone was going nuts. I flew out onto the deck straight into the arms of my brother, who was jumping up and down and screaming, "You did it, you did it!" I held on tight to my brother because my legs felt as if they might give out.

After landing the trick, Tom Boyle, a friend and pro I looked up to, came up and gave me a hug. He looked me straight in the eye and said, "I know exactly how you feel right now." I was sure he did because the fact is, only a skater knows that feeling.

right: Steve Alba taught me a lot about skating pools. Doubles in Garden Grove, California.

Media with an Attitude

Not everybody was convinced that my victory at the '96 X Games was anything very special. I realized this a few days later when I watched the taped event on television. The tone of the show made it clear that everyone at ESPN believed my win was a fluke. (And why shouldn't they? After all, I wasn't even sure that it wasn't.) Even in the end, when I beat Tony, they showed this short interview with me and then cut right to Tony for an in-depth analysis of the upset. (This wasn't Tony's fault; he had no idea they'd cut the tape like that.) This attitude caught on throughout the press and held on through the next season as well.

Thrasher magazine, the first skate magazine I had read as a kid, was now one of the publications that loved to put me down. The year after my X Games win, I was surprised by a phone call from the magazine requesting an interview. I was leery, but the writer swore that he wanted to give me a chance to respond to all the criticism I'd received from the magazine. The idea was kind of interesting, so I agreed.

The first criticism was, "You skate too much." Well, I just laughed and told him that was a compliment, not a criticism.

Then he went on to list other silly criticisms, like "You don't party enough" and "You're too friendly" and "You're a trick robot." I tried to explain that I am who I am, but it's hard to be serious about these kinds of comments.

When he made the claim "You're a big nerd," I had to agree. I said, "I don't argue with that one. I'm a total nerd. Nerds rule. They're the only ones who know that they're just geeks, and they're out to have fun, not to be cool. I'm definitely not trying to be someone I'm not."

Then he said, "You're a trainer." This criticism came from the fact that I work hard at skating and don't drink or smoke. I told him that I didn't work out or lift weights. I told him the truth: I just loved to skate. I admitted that some people may see that as training, but I was just having fun and learning new stuff. At the end I added sarcastically, "Really, I run five miles a day and eat a dozen raw eggs rampside." Of course, next to my picture in the article, that's the quote the editor used as a blown-up outtake.

Believe half of what you hear and nothing of what you read. The media will print or say whatever they want to—made up or not. This is something I had to learn to ignore. I can't let what the press or TV announcers or even other skaters say about me affect what I do or who I am. I'm not saying this is easy to do, but as long as my friends and family support me, I don't really care what anybody else thinks.

Keep on Pushin'

The pressure from the media really began to build up in the month before the '97 X Games. Tony won the first year and I won the second. To the press, this was the rubber match. They didn't have the faintest idea of what skateboarding was all about. They didn't get it that skateboarders aren't competitive in the same way that other athletes are. Everybody knows one another and we're really friendly during contests. Tony and I were never, and never would be, enemies. Over the years we had gotten to know each other when we traveled together for our mutual sponsors, like Swatch and Airwalk. There was no way we would let the media turn this into a grudge match between us.

But with only one year to get used to the pressure of people expecting me to win, I was nervous when the Games came around. I had just quit Human, my bread-and-butter board sponsor, and I was putting pressure on myself to do well so it would be easier to find a new sponsor.

I ended up being too nervous to skate. I dropped in for qualifiers and went for the hardest line I could. I had no strategy. I fell on flip tricks during both runs and ended up in fourteenth place, missing the cut by a long shot. Looking back, I realize that had I just cruised a standard run, I probably would have qualified. I felt so defeated. The way I saw it, I had let down not only myself, but also my father and all those people who had come to expect me to do well. It was like the time at gymnastics camp when I fell on my face, only a hundred times worse. It was the first time I had failed to qualify in the top ten since I'd turned pro. Chalk that one up to experience.

Tony and I won the doubles contest the very next day in what was one of the most enjoyable competitions I've ever skated in.

We had skated doubles many times before at demos, but this was the first time doubles skating was included in a contest. Tony and I were just on. We even showed up wearing T-shirts of the same color. After a good laugh Tony changed his shirt so we wouldn't look like total kooks in the "couples" contest. (Now it's common for guys in doubles contests to wear matching shirts and make up team names for the announcers to use. It's all in good fun.)

The real win for me in '97 was the street contest. Earlier that year I had landed my first back flip on a skateboard—thanks to the foam pits at Woodward Camp. I had tried it for a while in practice over the jump box, but I couldn't get the speed I needed. At the end of my second run in the street finals, just before the buzzer, I landed it—the first back flip ever to be done in competition! I placed second to Chris Senn, and it was just enough to help me feel better about my bad showing in the vert contest.

Getting Back Up

Missing the cut in vert at the X Games gave me a new form of motivation. My dad said, "You can't win 'em all," as dads do, but he went on to say that I was just going to have to go to the World Cup the next weekend in Münster, Germany, and win there. So I did just that. I went on that year to win more contests than any season since. By the year's end I'd won the overall vert title, placed second overall in street and won the combined overall championship title for the second year. Losing at the X Games turned out to be a blessing in disguise. At the time I thought it was the worst thing that could have happened to my career. But, as is my style, the face of adversity just made me try harder. Lesson #792: Keep skating, keep living, keep learning.

Things were also getting better in my life off the ramp. Although I still didn't have a board sponsor, I was winning enough contests to feel more financially independent. I bought a used (but new to me!) 1995 Honda Civic that started up every time I turned the key. Rhino, Preston, and I managed to move to an apartment without any roaches or termites. I didn't have a bed yet, but I used wood from an old fence and built this little loft over my desk where I could sleep. The most obvious sign that I was moving up in the world was the fact that I could eat out. About three times a week I'd grab a meal at Ranchos, a Mexican place down the street from my house. This was definitely an improvement over stealing finger food during happy hour at the Red Onion.

The only thing that I still wanted and didn't have was a new board sponsor. I wanted to skate for a company that was secure and established in the industry. After skating my best year ever, I finally got sponsored by Powell. Powell's Bones Brigade was the team I had wanted to ride for since I was a kid. They offered me a salary, along with health and dental benefits, for being a pro for them. Now I didn't have to worry about how I was going to pay for the airfare to or the hotel at the next contest. All I had to think about was skateboarding.

A Confidence Boost

In what I do, confidence is everything. No matter how many times I hear someone say, "You can do it!" I can't do my best until I believe it so strongly in myself that no one can knock me down with words. I learned to say, "You can't bring me down" as a mantra during rough times. I would repeat it in my head or even say it under my breath whenever things weren't going right or someone was vibing me. The '96 X Games and the '97 World Cup in Münster gave me the extra confidence boost I needed—proof that I could make it. Pop tells me that from that point on, I skated every contest as if I knew I could win if I wanted to.

I've kept that lesson with me to this day. It sounds cheesy, but you have to believe in yourself. The way you think about yourself as a skateboarder affects the way you can skate. Just recently, I tried a trick on the ramp for a half hour until I made it. It's totally a mental game. I did this trick easily before I had my knee and ankle operation, but it took me a while to do it again afterward. Now some days I can do it on the third try, and other days it takes me hours to get it once. It has nothing to do with my body's ability and even less to do with skill; it's all

mental. To make it, I have to decide before I drop in that this is going to be the one. Sometimes it works, and sometimes it doesn't; but I have to go for it knowing that I'll either land it or crash trying. There's no in-between.

previous spread: Gap ollie at a secret street spot in San Diego.

13.
it's all happening
It's still just skateboarding.

Whenever anyone asks me about my most memorable time as a skateboarder, I have to say it was between 1998 and 1999. Those were the years when I felt like I had really made it. I was winning important contests; I picked up some big endorsement deals; and I was finally doing nothing but skating for a living. And to top it off, Rebecca and I fell in love again.

Getting Better All the Time
The popularity of skateboarding was on the rise in the late '90s and the schedule of competitions became more packed. In 1995 there were about five pro contests a year. By 1996 that number had more than doubled. Summer was the "on season," and I spent it traveling back and forth from the States to Europe, South America, Asia, and Australia. The sport of skateboarding was seeing more exposure and more opportunities for

endorsements by athletes. I might be called to do a demo in Malaysia or to go to a contest in Australia. It was a great time to be a professional skateboarder.

In 1997, I started out with sponsors like Split Clothing and Airwalk. Over the next couple of years these deals brought more deals. I did commercials for The Gap, Sprite, and Lee jeans. I eventually hired an agent, John Flanagan, who helped me interpret all the contracts. I signed endorsement deals with some big names like SoBe Beverages and LEGO. I got my own video game with MTV Sports, a signature Big Air Straight Jump toy with Tech Deck, and I started my own Web site, andymacdonald.com. My image was on a United States Postal Service stamp as part of their "Extreme Sports" series. And in 2001, I had a signature watch with Swatch, and everyone in my family got watches that year for Christmas.

It seems like it all happened so fast, but when I look back on all those years, I knew it was a long time coming.

success without excess

Powell was paying me well and giving me health benefits, and I was making good money winning contests and doing demos. For the first time in my life I actually knew where the money was coming from to pay my bills. I have to admit that having money is good for peace of mind, but I never wanted it to define who I am or what I value. I always liked the simple life and didn't need too many material things to be happy—that didn't change when I finally had some dollars in my pocket.

One of the first things I bought when the money started coming in was Cinnamon Toast Crunch cereal. I love cereal, and it's always been a major part of my diet. It doesn't take a lot of effort to prepare, and I've never been much of a cook. When I lived on the floor at Bacon's and when I got my first roach-infested apartment, I couldn't afford more than bargain-brand raisin bran. If I ever had a little extra money for groceries, I would splurge on my favorite cereal—Cinnamon Toast Crunch. For me, this was a sure measure of success. When things weren't going so well and I didn't know where the next paycheck was coming from, like when I quit riding for Human, I'd go back to eating bargain-brand raisin bran until things got better. That's where I got what I call "raisin bran mentality." I don't need fancy cars or expensive things to prove I've made it. Even with thousands of people watching me at contests and with TV coverage and big sponsors and blah-blah-blah, when you get right down to it, it's still just skateboarding. It happens to be my living now, but I still do it because it's the most enjoyable, self-fulfilling thing that I know how to do. A large box of Cinnamon Toast Crunch says it all for me. It really doesn't take much.

Top-Gun Dudes

The week before the '98 X Games, Tony Hawk and I agreed to do a promotion for the U.S. Marines, which was sponsoring the Games. In this promo we would get to fly in F-18 military jets. I couldn't pass up this once-in-a-lifetime chance, but it wasn't as easy as showing up and just doing it. To prepare, we had to go through four days of intensive flight training.

The first few days were spent in classrooms learning how to use emergency equipment. The hardest part for me came on the last day in the helo-dunker. After my near-drowning experiences while surfing, this could have been the deal breaker for me if Tony hadn't convinced me to stick with it. The instructor explained that we would be strapped into the simulated belly of a helicopter, which would drop from a twelve-foot platform into a fifteen-foot-deep pool and then flip upside down as it sank to the bottom. Wearing all of our gear (flight helmet, combat boots, flight suit, survival vest, and life vest), we would have to unstrap ourselves, get out of the copter, and find our way to the surface of the water.

I was told to wait for the copter to completely flip over before exiting, but on my first try, when it was only halfway around, I was out of there. So we all had to do it again. I got it right that time but found out we had to do it a third and a fourth time—blindfolded. They weren't kidding! By the time I found my way out of the copter, I was already almost out of breath. So I swam as hard as I could, hoping I was heading in the right direction. When I broke through the top of the water, I was gasping for air like a man one second away from drowning.

Fortunately, Tony and I both passed the tests and were psyched to be able to fly. We were going up as the co-pilots in separate planes for an hour and a half. My goal during this mission was to stay conscious without throwing up or passing out (which can easily happen taking turns at supersonic speeds). The G-force was so great that it pulled the skin on my face back and pulled my eyelids down. And there was no way I could lift my arms up. This made even the most difficult skateboard trick look pretty simple. It was fun, but I was glad when we were back on the ground. This was one of those death-defying experiences that has become part of my best memories.

'98 X Games

A week after my top-gun adventure I was back in more comfortable surroundings at the '98 X Games in San Diego. I had just moved from a rent-controlled apartment into a real house that I bought in Ocean Beach. My pop and stepmom and even Rebecca had all come out to see me compete. I was having so much fun that I wasn't at all focused on the contest. I even showed up forty-five minutes late for doubles practice with Tony. He was stressing!

"What, dude?" I said, laughing. "We've got it."

At least I thought we had it until I forgot one of my runs during the qualifying rounds. As we stood on the deck waiting to go I started to get our first run and our second run confused. I asked Tony, "What's after the ally oop?"

"There is no ally oop in this run!" he said.

Before I could think, it was time to drop in. I knew we were in trouble. I just blanked. We ended up just popping out on the deck looking at each other like, *Now what?*

Even though I messed up one line completely, we still made the cut with our next run and went on to win the gold again in the finals. I also won gold in the vert and a silver in street with some of the most confident skating I've ever done. It was a great contest. I wasn't nervous at all, and the whole thing just seemed like no big deal. I was so relaxed that year that I fell asleep on a table just before my street runs. Life was good—two golds and a silver, a new house, and a "new" girlfriend.

right: This was the photo they used for the cover of my first video game. Japan air at Mission Valley.

My Future Wife—Again

Rebecca and I had kept in touch on and off over the years. She had left Eureka after a year and went back to get her college degree at the University of Massachusetts Amherst. She spent some time in Paris and then jumped right back into my life.

In 1998 she called me out of the blue, wondering who she should talk to to get a job at Woodward Camp. I hooked her up with the right person, and she was hired for the summer as the recreation director for the skate and bike kids. We planned for her to come out to California for a visit in July before the X Games. I was having a housewarming party, and I wanted her to be there, so I bought her a plane ticket.

Rebecca stayed with me and my family at my new house, and as the week went by we fell in love all over again. This was it. No wonder I couldn't keep my mind on skating!

Two years later I asked Rebecca to marry me. And then, after winning the vert at the 2000 NBC Gravity Games in Providence, Rhode Island, our families finally met each other. I wanted everyone to know that I had found the one person I wanted to spend the rest of my life with. The older I get, the more amazing that becomes to me. I know people who have spent their whole lives looking and waiting for that one person to come along. Not a day goes by when I don't feel like the luckiest person in the world to have found Rebecca—again.

We married on March 31, 2001, and a year later became the proud parents of a chocolate Labrador puppy named Nishi. I think she might be the best dog in the world.

A World Record

The fun just kept coming in 1999. After I moved to California, I would sometimes spend part of my summers at Windell's Snowboard Camp in Mt. Hood, Oregon. The camp had huge, oversized jumps there that we used to call "superkickers." You had to straightline from the top of the hill and hit the long drawn-out kicker; there was a sixty-foot gap that you had to clear, and the landing was a steep bank of snow that you couldn't see until you were airborne. I finally got up the courage to try it, and when I did it without killing myself, I realized that I loved the feeling of flying. I knew it would be even better on a skateboard.

But how could I get the money to build a superkicker skate-boarding ramp?

I mentioned my idea to my sponsor Swatch. I knew they wouldn't hand over money just so I could have some fun, so I hyped the idea a bit. "I think," I told them, "that I could set a world record for the longest distance jump on a skateboard." They saw right away that this would bring Swatch lots of attention. Personally, I didn't much care about setting a record; I just wanted to see if this kind of thing would even be possible on a skateboard.

Swatch bought the idea and gave me some money. I hired Tim Paine, a well-known ramp builder, to help me, and we began building in a friend's backyard in Lansing, Michigan. No one had ever done this before, so we had no idea what to do. But, just like with my old Melrose ramps, we tried one thing, and if that didn't look right, we tried another. On October 12, 1999, we had a 300-foot-long, Evel Knievel–style ramp that was thirty-six feet high. The drop-in was only four feet wide, and it swayed in the breeze. I had run out of money to make it any wider, so it was going to have to do. To be honest, I was scared to death. If I fell on the drop-in or came up short on the jump, it was all over. Still, I couldn't wait to try it.

We parked four cars in the gap between the ramps for effect. As I made each jump we pulled the landing ramp back farther and farther. I took a couple of good hippers, but it was well worth it. It was the closest I'll ever come to actually flying. I did a 360 that was about forty-seven feet long, which had to be the scariest yet most fun thing I've ever done in my life. To do a 360, you have to turn your back to the landing, so I was blindsided for a while, looking down at the roofs of the cars below. That's not something I was used to seeing—but I guess that's what made it so exciting.

Somehow I got the idea in my head that I wanted to go over fifty feet. (I think it was my dad's idea.) Tim and I tacked a four-by-eight sheet of plywood to the top of the starting ramp, but we didn't have time to make it a roll-in. The ramp was now forty-one feet high and I was going for a record tail drop as well. Just like when I dropped in on a half pipe for the first time, I concentrated on not thinking about what I was about to do. I climbed to the top, grabbed the two-by-four we had tacked to the side for balance (there was no time for railings either), clicked my tail out over the edge, and dropped in. A fifty-two-foot, ten-inch jump put me in the *Guinness Book of World Records.* The distance, though, really has nothing to do with it; the feeling of flying and being in the air long enough to do tricks the sport has never seen is what makes the straight jump so awesome. I see these ramps being built more in the future for straight jump best trick competitions. Why not create a new discipline in skateboard contests?

Skating at the White House

I soon found out that being a pro skater has perks even off the ramps. One of these was when I got to ride on the smooth marble floors of the White House.

I remember well the old "frying pan" anti-drug ads I saw on TV as a kid. In 1998, when I saw people I admire like Chuck D and Lauryn Hill, appearing in new, much cooler antidrug ads, I thought I'd like to do one too. I contacted the Partnership for a Drug-Free America and became the first athlete the organization ever used in a public service announcement.

After my commercial debuted, I was talked into giving a five-minute speech to introduce the POTUS (President of the United States, in White House lingo) at a press conference. I'd never done any public speaking, and this didn't seem to be the best place to give it a try. But like any skateboarder might say, *If you're gonna go, go big.* So I agreed.

As I walked through the White House on the morning of my speech, I felt great. I was sure that I was the first guy to walk through the front door with a skateboard under his arm, and I just had to set it down and roll down the hall a bit. The Secret Service agents were not nearly as pleased about it as I was. Before the press conference I had a chance to meet with President Clinton and give him an Andy Macdonald T-shirt and a signed board with my graphic on it. Then, before I knew it, I was being hustled onto a stage alongside the president in front of about 350 reporters, including C-SPAN's live coverage. *What am I doing here?* I thought. *I'm not one of these suits!* I was wearing a pair of cargoes and a plaid shirt.

As I sat down next to President Clinton I tried to remind myself to relax. It was no use. I got more nervous as each

above: My speech at the White House was the first real public speaking I'd ever done.

speaker before me finished. (I don't even get this nervous after falling on my first run at a contest.) The president nudged me with his elbow, took a deep breath, and exhaled—suggesting that I do the same. As I stepped up to the podium I had a little trouble pulling my speech from the pocket of my cargoes. I made a funny face exaggerating my troubles, and a few people laughed. Then I gave a little disclaimer stating that I was not a public speaker and was not used to this "meet the president" stuff. To my surprise and relief, everyone began laughing and clapping. I realized that they were just people and not some strange government breed I couldn't relate to. That made me feel a little more relaxed, but I was still glad when it was over. As I sat back down in my chair, President Clinton started his speech saying, "That was great, Andy. Maybe you should go into politics after you're done skateboarding." I don't think I'll ever take him up on that suggestion, but I appreciated the compliment.

When I handed in my visitor's pass at the front gate, I realized that it might be a very long time, if ever, before I walked through those doors again. But I felt good. I had pulled off the speech and felt like I'd done something important by speaking out against drugs. But most of all, I felt I had done something special to help pave the way for future generations of kids who love skateboarding as much as I do.

The Hot Seat

After my day with Bill, I got an opportunity to be on *The Tonight Show*. The crew wanted me to make a grand entrance on my board. So when I was introduced, I came out skating and ollied up onto Jay Leno's desk before sitting down in the hot seat. "Your mom must love it when you come home for dinner," Leno joked.

Leno wanted me to skate during the show, so his crew had built some ramps for me to play around on. There were lights, cameras, and the audience crowding the takeoff and landing. It was pretty sketchy. To add to the challenge, we decided that, like Evel Knievel, I would jump over something—oh, a dozen XFL cheerleaders should be good.

I was nervous waiting my turn on the show. But once I got on my board and entered the set, it was just another interview (which I was finally used to by now!). The whole experience was a lot of fun, and it was one of those moments that made up for all the years of put-downs, turndowns, prejudice, hunger, and poverty. Through good times and bad, I've always loved being a skateboarder.

14.

the future of skateboarding

*You're skaters; you're extreme, and you don't know any better. Well, we
do know better.*

It's been ten years since I left home to become a professional
skateboarder. A lot has changed since that time. Back then there
were only a handful of skaters in each town. According to
American Sports Data, there are now more than eighteen million
skateboarders in the United States! Today there are more kids
skateboarding than playing baseball.

The change has also been personal: I made it. I'm a pro
skater, living out my dreams and getting paid to do what I love.
I came off knee and ankle surgery at the end of 2001 and won
the first three contests I entered. I received an award from
World Cup Skateboarding for being the six-time "Overall World
Champion." I still travel a lot with my sponsors. In 2002 alone,
I went to Italy, South Africa, France, Denmark, Germany,
Switzerland, and Austria. I now have my own line of Andy Mac
branded products, ranging from shoes and clothing to skateboards

and safety equipment. I even helped design the next generation of the pogo stick called the Flybar. And on top of all this, skateboarding is still the most enjoyable thing I know how to do.

Here to Stay

Some people insist that skateboarding is just a fad. I don't think so. Every year I see more and more kids out there cheering on their favorite skateboarders. At the 2002 ESPN X Games in Philadelphia, there were nearly 300,000 fans. Even still, there are some skeptics who say that attendance is high because action sports don't charge an admission fee. But in 2002, for the first time, admission was charged at the Gravity Games in Ohio, and it sold out four hours before practice even started.

Skateboarding may be becoming even more popular because most mainstream sports seem to have forgotten about their fans. Many families can't even afford a night out at the ballpark, never mind getting an autograph from your favorite player while you're there. By contrast, the majority of skateboarding events are free, and pro skateboarders continue to be some of the most accessible athletes there are.

I admit that there have been cycles of popularity (the lowest was the year I arrived in California!). But the sport has always come back, and now it's stronger than ever. Parents today aren't completely clueless because they're more likely to have grown up with their own skateboards in the garage. And skateparks are now more accessible. In 1999 there were only about 300 public skateboard parks in America. By 2003 that number was near 2,000. More and more kids everywhere are giving it a try.

Along with the increase in popularity, there are now more contests, more prize money, more willing sponsors, and, therefore, more opportunities to make a living skateboarding. Being a professional skateboarder is not such a crazy idea anymore— it's a legitimate career choice.

Corporate Sellout?

One of the reasons I can make a living as a skateboarder is because I have corporate sponsors who pay me to advertise their products. Most pros do. Today I am supported by big-name companies such as SoBe Beverages, Swatch, and LEGO. Other

skaters have the backing of companies such as AT&T, Taco Bell, Target, Apple Computers, and Ford Motor Company, and they endorse such products as Hot Wheels, Mountain Dew, Right Guard, and Bagel Bites, to name only a few. Unfortunately, some people see the downfall of skateboarding in this kind of "sellout" to large corporations.

Skateboarders are historically an independent group who have never wanted to be tied to big business. Some say that I shouldn't be making a profit off of the sport—that to remain the art form that it is, skateboarding should stay in the streets and backyards, where it started. But I know that as long as I'm being true to what I believe in, that's all that really matters. I pride myself on making sure that the sponsors I choose give something back to the sport that has given me so much. For example, before I signed with LEGO, I convinced them to sponsor the California Amateur Skateboard League. Sonja Catalano, the woman who runs the CASL, came up to me at an event and gave me a big hug. "Thank you so much," she said. "LEGO's been the best sponsor. We've had more success this year than ever." Corporate sponsors are the reason many more of us can make a living doing something we love. Compared to any other sport, pro skateboarders are still just getting started. If I had wanted to be rich, I would've played golf.

what's a skateboarder?

Some people think skateboarders should be hardcore, dirty, and edgy—and I'm not. I'm just me. I don't have tattoos, piercings, or even long hair. I don't smoke, drink, do drugs, or even drink coffee. Does this make me bad for skateboarding? Does this mean that I may influence other kids and that we'll end up with a whole generation of skaters who don't do drugs? I hope so, but I don't know. I do hope that future skateboarders will be happy to be who they are and won't feel they have to change to match someone else's image. That, after all, is one of the reasons we all started skating in the first place. That's what being

previous spread: The scariest thing and the most fun thing I've ever done on my skateboard: world record straight jump in Lansing, Michigan.

a "punk skater" is all about. At first people dyed their hair blue or wore a Mohawk because nobody else did; it was an expression of individuality. But today tattoos and body piercings are the norm, and they're not so unique or individual anymore. The most punk-rock thing you can do is to be yourself and never waver from your beliefs—even when others put you down. By this logic, I think Gandhi was the most punk-rock man who ever lived. If he had skated, he would have ripped!

Skate Moms

Some people worry that skateboarding will be ruined when soccer moms turn their vans around and start heading to the skateparks. They worry that parents will start organizing little skateboard teams with adult coaches. I see that happening already in some places, but I'm not worried. I know that skateboarding at its roots is here to stay, and even all the world's over-involved parents put together can't kill its spirit.

It's true that skateboarding started in kids' backyards and on public streets, but just because its popularity now brings it to skateparks and large, arena-sponsored competitions doesn't mean it's doomed. No matter how big and mainstream the sport gets, it will always begin with kids hanging out and having fun. There will always be kids out on the street with their skateboards just because they love the feeling they get from rolling. They'll find backyard pools whether there are cameras around or not. It will always have that personal, independent element because that's the essence of skateboarding.

Skaters Unite

There is a new development in skateboarding that will help pro skateboarders get the respect and benefits that other athletes enjoy in this country. It is a new organization called the United Professional Skateboarders Association (UPSA). In the beginning of 2001, I realized that I was tired of fighting by myself for better treatment from the television networks. I was tired of being taken advantage of by companies that were cashing in on the sport's popularity but could care less about it. They were making a load of money off the televised contests ($30 million in advertising

dollars alone for one show!) and giving back less than one percent to the athletes. By comparison, members of the National
Football League Players Association receive seventy percent of
the money that comes in from each game.

Along with other skateboarders, I was ready to take a stand
at the 2001 ESPN X Games in Philadelphia. ESPN had new contracts for all the athletes to sign. Not only would we forfeit the
usual rights to our "name and likeness in perpetuity throughout
the universe," but we would agree to give Disney the right to use
everyone's image without any payment in an upcoming IMAX
movie.

"Hold on," I said. "I'm a member of the Screen Actors Guild,
and I can't be in a movie unless you're paying me SAG rates.
And when have you heard of anyone, even an extra, being in a
movie without being paid?"

We hired a sports attorney to represent us. She talked to the
ESPN lawyers, and they agreed to take the clause out of the
contracts. Then the night before the Games, they changed their
mind. We spent that night writing up a press release announc-
ing the boycott of the X Games: If that clause remained, we
weren't skating.

Buster Halterman, another active UPSA member, and I
showed up early the next morning at the First Union Center in
Philadelphia, where the Games were being held. As other
skateboarders began arriving we showed them the clauses in
the contract that we were protesting. It didn't take long for
every single skater to agree that we would stand together and
refuse to go in to practice until they fixed our contract.
Eventually, a bigwig from ESPN came out to talk to us.

"If you don't take out the clause," I said, "we're not skating."

"Fine, then I guess you're not skating," he said, and walked
away.

At that moment I knew I had come a long way. I remembered the day I pushed my homemade ramp up to my mom's
station wagon and hoped I could make the jump without killing
myself or wrecking her car. Now I was sacrificing more than
my own body or an old Datsun. My career was on the line. My

left: I love teaching kids how to drop in.

ability to make a living depended on these contests and on the sponsors who expected me to skate them. But at that moment it was more important to me to stand up for the rights of all skateboarders who were getting taken advantage of. It was more important to stand up against the people who thought, *Hey, you're skaters; you're extreme, and you'll be in an IMAX movie for free because you don't know any better.* Well, we do know better.

All the skaters stayed tight, and our lawyer told ESPN that if we didn't reach an agreement by 10:00 A.M. we would go to the press with our release, explaining why the skaters weren't in the X Games. We knew that Philly is a strong union town and that we'd have the support of the public. ESPN knew it too and didn't want any bad press. Fifteen minutes later ESPN backed down and removed the clause from everyone's contract—the skaters, bikers, in-liners, rock climbers, and motor-cross dudes all benefited. There is definitely strength in numbers. It was a historic battle and the first time pro skateboarders showed real solidarity and came away with concrete results.

The UPSA can do a lot for skaters in the future. We want to continue to protect the rights of skaters—both their names and their images. I was in a discount department store a while ago, and I saw the face of my friend Donny Barley smiling at me from the front of a T-shirt. His name wasn't on it, but I recognized him. The picture was stolen from *Transworld Skateboarding* magazine and scanned onto a T-shirt without ever asking his permission. Someone was making money from these shirts, and Donny wasn't seeing a penny of it! In what other sport can you do that? This kind of thing just isn't right. We're working to make sure that doesn't happen anymore.

The UPSA is also working to provide medical and dental insurance for all professional skateboarders. With the kind of slams we put our bodies through, it's crazy that so many pro skaters don't even have health insurance. Someday maybe we'll also have a retirement plan and disability insurance—the kinds of things that the athletes in every other sport have. We are professional athletes; we, too, should be able to make a living and protect our future.

dangerous activities

Four years ago the International Association of Skateboard Companies petitioned in California to have skateboarding included on the list of dangerous activities. This sounds bad, but it's really a good thing. This changed the law and added skateboarding to a list that includes soccer, football, Frisbee, kite flying, and tree climbing. This means that if you're skateboarding on a city street and fall and break your arm, you can't sue the city, because you were involved in what is considered "a dangerous activity" of your own choice. Before skateboarding was added to this list, cities didn't want skateparks or street riding because they knew they could be sued when a kid got hurt. Now they're not as worried. Almost every other state in the nation has followed this lead, and the result is a wave of skateboard park construction all over the country. This has been good for skaters, but it's hard to ignore that skating is still illegal on most city streets. Imagine if kids were given tickets for throwing a football outside of a football field or for bouncing a basketball down the street. Even though some things are looking better, there's still a lot to do.

Living the Dream

Some people say I'm lucky, but I don't think so. I don't remember anything lucky happening to me all those years I was struggling to become a pro skateboarder. Instead of *lucky,* I'd call myself *determined.* I've always known what I wanted to do, so I worked hard, I practiced, and I would never give up or give in—even when everyone else said I was crazy.

Now, every day that I'm not traveling, I slide down the twenty-six-foot fire pole I installed in my house. I head out to my backyard to bounce on my trampoline. Then I grab my skateboard and head outside or to the park to skate. As long as I just keep doing what I'm doing, people pay me to ride my skateboard—and that's all I've ever wanted.

Sometimes I lie in bed at night and think, *I can't believe this is all mine. I can't believe that skateboarding has bought me a house, a car, the gallon of milk in the fridge, and all the boxes of*

Cinnamon Toast Crunch I want. To this day, my dream come true still feels like a dream.

If I've learned one thing in my life so far it's to chase your dreams no matter how crazy they may seem. I did.

I told you so.

right: Tweaked slob air at the Triple Crown in Chicago, Illinois.

glossary

540: one and half rotations of your body and board in the air; originally done by Mike McGill, grabbing mute, and called a "McTwist"

air: any time you fly above the lip of a ramp while grabbing your board

alley-oop backside air: a backside air in which you approach the lip of the ramp as if you're going frontside, then turn backside, traveling across the ramp in the opposite direction of a standard backside air

backside air: an air in which your back is toward the deck of the ramp and you're grabbing the board with your front hand on the heel edge

backside grab: grabbing with your front hand on your heel edge while turning backside

backside grind: sliding ("grinding") with your back truck (axle) on an edge with your back facing that edge

backside revert: as you start to descend the ramp riding forward, you spin a backside 180 as you come down the transition, sliding your wheels toward your heels and finish the trick riding fakie (backward)

boardslide: sliding on your board between the two trucks (axles)

body wrap lien to tail, (a.k.a. "Mummy"): a trick I invented when I was a kid; it's a frontside air in which you pass the board behind your back before landing on the lip of the ramp on your tail just before riding back down

Christ air: a backside air in which you take the board off your feet and extend your legs and arms like a cross; invented and named by Christian Hosoi

fakie: riding backward

flip tricks: anytime the board flips under your feet before you land on it again

frontside grind to tail: a grind in which your body faces the edge you're grinding, then you turn another 90 degrees, smacking your tail on the edge before riding away

frontside invert: approaching the lip frontside, you grab the board with your back hand, planting your front hand on the lip, and do a one-handed handstand before coming back into the ramp

indy grab: grabbing your board on your toe edge with your back hand while going backside

kickflip: an ollie or air in which you kick with your front foot off the heel edge of your board to flip it over once before landing on it

kickflip indy: kick flipping into a backside air on a ramp, then grabbing indy

kickturn grind: a 180-degree turn in which all of your weight is still in the ramp, but your back truck grinds the lip for a second

mute grab blunt 180: you stall on the lip of the ramp, resting on your back truck and tail, grab with your front hand on your toe edge, and hop a backside 180 back into the ramp

ollie: jumping into the air with the board on your feet, without grabbing it with your hands; originally done in 1978 by Alan "Ollie" Gelfand

ollie blunt: stalling on the lip of a ramp between your back truck and your tail, then ollieing back into the ramp

ollie grab: an ollie where, once in the air, you grab your board

slob fast plant: touching your back foot quickly off the lip of the ramp before jumping into an air, grabbing with your front hand on your toe edge, going frontside

thread-the-needle air: a backside air in which you pass the board between your legs (from backside grab to indy grab) before coming back in

tweaked air: any air in which you pull or push your body's position in the air to the fullest extent as if doing a stretch

varial air: any air in which the board is spun 180 degrees with your hand, so the front of the board becomes the back

right: Lien to tail on makeshift extension at Encinitas.

© RHINO